RAINBOW AFTER RAIN

Books by Janet Lambert

Dear Readers:

Mother always said she wanted her books to be good enough to be found in someone's attic!

After all of these years, I find her stories—not in attics at all—but prominent in fans' bookcases just as mine are. It is so heart-warming to know that through these republications she will go on telling good stories and being there for her "girls," some of whom find no other place to turn.

    With a heart full of love and pride–
    Janet Lambert's daughter,
      Jeanne Ann Vanderhoef

RAINBOW
AFTER RAIN

BY

Janet Lambert

❦

Image Cascade Publishing

www.ImageCascade.com

MANUFACTURED IN THE UNITED STATES
OF AMERICA

A hardcover edition of this book was originally published by E. P. Dutton & Co. It is here reprinted by arrangement with Mrs. Jeanne Ann Vanderhoef.

First *Image Cascade Publishing* edition published 2000.
Copyright renewed © 1981 by Jeanne Ann Vanderhoef

Library of Congress Cataloging in Publication Data
Lambert, Janet 1895-1973
    Rainbow after rain.

(Juvenile Girls)
Reprint. Originally published: New York: E. P. Dutton, 1953.

ISBN 978-1-930009-22-6

For

L I N D A

RAINBOW AFTER RAIN

CHAPTER 1

"Miss Parrish. Hey, Miss Parrish! There's a telephone call for you."

The girl who usually sat at the switchboard poked her head around a corner of the long corridor. Tippy skidded to a stop before the door to an office that she considered partly hers. She had a desk in there to use, when she had time to sit down; and she slapped a plastic mixing bowl and an egg beater on it so she could reach across for the black instrument that yelped orders to her all day long, from wherever her boss happened to be. But her sister's voice floated blithely over the wire.

"Hi," it said. "How are you?"

"Oh, Penny!" Tippy slid into a leather desk chair and answered with a rush, "Don't you know you aren't supposed to call me up? I'm only an errand girl. TV stations are fussy and we have a show going on at three o'clock." Then she stopped and asked, "How did they ever happen to let you speak to me, anyway?"

"I have pull." Penny's voice held laughter as it went on, "I'm Penny Parrish, remember. I guest-starred on your station last week and I'm being besieged to do a program of my own. Right now I could ask to speak to a white mouse and the whole staff would go crawling around to find one for me. They're lucky that I only wanted you."

"Why, I never heard you brag like this." Tippy sat up straight on her chair and couldn't believe it was her very modest sister talking. Penny had always underrated her success as an actress; therefore she asked, "You aren't running a temperature, are you?"

"Nope. Want to lunch with me?"

"I can't."

"You can. Your boss said you could, so how about Patelli's, at one? I have something wonderful to tell you."

Tippy knew Penny's brown eyes were dancing. They danced right into the telephone, and the happy bubbles in her voice were what audiences paid a great deal of money to hear. She wasn't Mrs. Joshua MacDonald today, mother of two children, who had a lot on her mind; she was Penny Parrish, the star of *A Month of Sundays* and a motion picture, *One Step to Heaven,* that had broken records last year and won her a Hollywood award.

"Oh, all right," Tippy said, curious and wanting so much to go. "If Miss Turnbull will let me, that is."

"She will. One o'clock sharp. Bye, cherub."

Cherub. Tippy laid down the receiver and sat staring at it. Penny always called her cherub—and so had Ken. "Cherub," Ken had said, "when I come back from Korea we'll be married with a bang." But he hadn't come back. And even after a year-and-a-half of hopeless waiting, the sound of Penny saying cherub could twist her heart. Tippy pushed her short bright curls away from her face and rested her cheek in the palm of her hand with a sigh. For a moment she forgot that Studio One was waiting for a mixing bowl. She was suddenly lost again and lonely. High above New York with its rush and noisy commotion, its crush of people all trying to go somewhere, climbing to success like a lot of pygmies scaling a ladder, she was just a small, disappointed girl with no particular ambition, staring out at a summer sky.

Her hazel eyes held wistful sadness, and her soft lips pressed tightly together, twitching and winking the little dimples at the corners of her mouth without gaiety.

"Oh, me," he said to herself as she stood up. "I didn't mean to be unhappy again today. I promised myself this morning I wouldn't. I was really excited, driving in town with Dad, and eager for work and a date tonight. This is silly." She reached for her mixing bowl, dropped the egg beater and scooped it up. I wish I could be like Penny, she thought, charging along the corridor again. All sparkly and gay. Making people turn to look at me, just because I'm so wonderful.

The idea amused her, comparing herself to her vivid sister, so that she really flashed her twinkly dimples as she sailed along; and it would have surprised her to see how many heads did turn. Old Mr. Semple, who was in promotion, peered out of his cubicle, and young Graham Laughton, the sports commentator, straightened his tie. The new time salesman snatched up his brief case, suddenly remembering an errand that would take him toward the studios.

"Hello there," he said, catching up with Tippy as she mounted the circular iron staircase which led to a bustling world above. "I'm Paul Granger. I met you yesterday, remember?"

"Of course." She moved over to the rail to make room for him and came back to her present world. "You're on the Macklin account, aren't you?" she asked. "I'm just taking up some props for it. We have a scene in the kitchen today, and the long-lost Dania is coming back." She looked up at him as they spiraled, and he thought he had never seen such golden eyes. "Dania's been out of the script for three weeks," she said. "She left home one day and it looked as if the writers had forgotten all about her. But here she is again."

"Miss Parrish, you're speaking lightly of the soap opera I love." He leaped forward to open the heavy fire door for her, and asked as she went through, "How about lunch? Are you eating anywhere special?"

"With my sister. She invited me out in style."

Paul Granger knew who Tippy was. Word had gone around that she was related to the famous Penny Parrish, that her father was a retired army colonel, a friend of the president of WRIP-TV and a radio commentator on foreign affairs. Some of the underlings were jealous of her and said she had got her job through "pull." A few girls had bravely snubbed her when she started work five months ago, hoping to prove their contempt for anyone who had not come up the hard way, while others had openly fawned on her and watched to see what favors she received or what special crumbs they might nip up, simply by knowing her.

But Tippy received no favors. She drove in from the country with her father each morning but never had been known to see him again during the day. Sometimes people had heard her whisper, "Rest some today, Dad," when they left the elevator, and once, when his limp that came from a war wound was more noticeable than usual, she had stood with her eyes following his slow progress across the large carpeted lobby. But she had squared her shoulders and turned briskly away. Nothing was gained by knowing her, for she seemed to want nothing for herself. She ran her errands, took the blame from an irate producer when something went wrong on the set, and was Miss Turnbull's best girl Friday.

Now she said, "Oh, golly, I'm late with these things," and darted off.

The young man left behind wondered how one spoke more than two or three sentences to such a will-o'-the-wisp, but Tippy was too busy to inform him. She might have said: "Just drop in at our house up near the Hudson and sit around with Mums and Dad and me in the evenings, watching such a silly thing as television, or hunt me up over at my brother David's, or at Pen's on week ends, when she isn't playing and can laze around out at her own house. Or, most days, you might bring your own lunch and eat across the desk from me, any time from twelve o'clock to three, whenever I've fifteen minutes free." But she didn't. Miss Turnbull was rushing around like an old motorcycle out of control, and she forgot Paul Granger.

And it was five minutes after one before she was free to meet Penny.

"Well, for pity's sakes," Penny cried, jumping up from the chair where she had been sitting and spilling her purse and white gloves from her lap. "What kept you?"

"Work." Tippy bent to retrieve the gloves while Penny picked up her purse, and the blond head and the brown bumped smartly together. "Ouch," she said as they came up. "We need football helmets. I see you didn't wear a hat, either."

"Too hot."

Penny straightened her Shantung suit, fluffed bronze bangs back into place, and Tippy said enviously, "Even a pony tail doesn't look too silly on you, though why you tie your hair back that way is beyond me."

"I have to, pet, because of the play. It's either that or go around all day peeking out of a bush. I can stand it for an hour and forty-five minutes every night, but just try it on a hot August day. I wish I could have it as short as yours."

"Pooh!" Tippy dismissed her own natural curls that had always been worn short, and said without preamble, "I'm hungry. And I have to be back at two."

"Right. I have a table reserved, so start marching."

They followed a head waiter along a carpeted aisle, past

16

tables that held cool salads and ices, and over her shoulder Penny asked, "New dress?"

"Birthday present from Mums—in advance. Did you know," Tippy said, leaning forward a little, "I'll be twenty next month? I'm a big girl now, and next year I can vote. I work, too."

"And that," Penny answered, sliding into a chair held out for her, "is exactly what I brought you here to talk about."

"May I order first?"

The whole family had gone into huddles over Tippy's first job. It was the kind of family that went into huddles, on the slightest provocation, and so whatever Penny had to say could wait, for it would be nothing that hadn't been said a dozen times before. Each had asked in turn, "Are you sure, dear, this is what you really want for a career?" "Are you sure you won't mind getting up every morning at six o'clock?" "Are you sure you wouldn't rather go on to college for another year?" Tippy had nodded like a mandarin, was still nodding now and then, so she said, "I'd like that cold plate with turkey and ham and fruit salad. And iced tea, please."

"I'll have it, too." Penny gave back her unopened menu and leaned across the table. "Cherub," she said, smiling, and this time Tippy didn't even flinch, "I have the most exciting news. You just aren't going to believe it."

"Another baby?" Tippy smiled, too, but Penny switched her funny-looking tail of hair.

"What would I want with another baby?" she asked. And she went on without waiting for an answer, "I have Parrie almost ready for her first year in school, and Joshu's reached some sort of respectable walking and talking age—why should I want to start all over?"

"Search me," Tippy answered, and shrugged. "It's the way you've twice announced your blessed event, that's all."

"The news concerns *you*, my pet."

For one wild moment, Tippy thought Penny might have heard something of Ken. She half sat forward, then let herself drop back again. Ken had died in a hospital. All his belongings had been returned. *"The personal possessions of Lieutenant Kenneth Prescott are hereby. . . ."* "What concerns me, Pen?" she asked.

"A part in my new play."

The answer was so astounding that Tippy could only stare.

"A part," Penny repeated. "It's just a little one, but Josh says you can do it. He's such a wonderful director and he can coach you on the side."

"My friend," Tippy's senses were beginning to return and she wanted to laugh, right into Penny's young eager enthusiasm, but she went on, "Josh may be able to make a monkey talk, but he couldn't get me on the stage and off again, even if I only had to say, 'Madam, dinner is served.' I'm no actress."

"But Josh could turn you into one. He's a producer. He's also the best director in the business, and he's. . . ."

"He's your husband. But, no thank you."

"Oh, Tippy!"

Penny looked down at the plate a waiter set before her as

if wondering what it was and what it was doing there, but Tippy picked up her fork with businesslike purpose. "I'd be fine in a play with you," she said. "As soon as the lights came up after the first-act curtain, people would grab their programs to see who that awful girl was. Imagine their surprise when they read down the line: 'Joshua MacDonald presents Penny Parrish in Something-or-other, a play by Someone-or-other. Cast of characters in order of their appearance—Somebody-or-other, Somebody-or-other! And suddenly—wham! 'Andrea Parrish.' 'My soul,' they'd yelp, 'it can't be! Do you suppose that horror belongs in the family?'"

"Oh, they wouldn't."

"And they'd shake their heads at each other and mutter, 'It beats the Dutch. Husband's always the producer, wife's the star—and now the little sister's muddling along. I wonder when they're going to drag in Colonel and Mrs. Parrish, and the brother who's a West Point cadet. Of course they still have another brother and his wife, and if they could use a batch of children, they have those, too.'"

"Tippy, stop it."

"Well, it's what they'd say." Tippy took a bite of salad, washed it down with iced tea to add further, "It's what *I* say. Thank you very much, but, no."

"We could change your name," Penny persisted, undaunted and determined. "There are lots of good ones left in the family. How about Mum's maiden name? Andrea Avery?"

"It sounds as if I'm about to take off and fly. I couldn't do it, Pen. Thanks, loads, but I couldn't. I'd die of fright."

19

Penny picked up her own fork then laid it down again. She wanted so much to do something for this little sister who had had her world jerked out from under her. Tippy had known so well what she wanted from life, which was marriage with Ken. Penny looked across at the fluffy head bent over a plate, at long dark lashes covering eyes that were often too sad and serious. "Tippy," she asked gently, "has it ever occurred to you that life bopped you one because you were too young for what you wanted?"

"Sometimes." Tippy looked up without surprise. She knew how Penny's thoughts ran, and she went on, "I know I was too young to fall in love with Ken when I did. I was only sixteen when it began and he was an officer. If I'd been going around with boys my own age I wouldn't have known him. I've pointed all that out to myself, Pen. But Germany was a lonely place. And there I was, in the Army of Occupation, with just Mums and Dad for companionship. I grew up pretty fast, you see."

She smiled and, because the problem of her sorrow was one she had gone over many times in her own mind and understood and lived with, she dismissed it and returned to the original discussion. "Don't worry about me, Pen," she begged earnestly. "I'm not unhappy now, the way I was last winter. I'll always love Ken, but there are days and days when I don't think of him at all. I'm so very busy, you see. And I do thank you for inviting me to ruin your new play. It was sweet, and just like you."

"You won't do it?"

"Silly, of course not." She gestured at her plate with her

fork, remarked, "This is a very good lunch, by the way," and resumed her eating.

There was nothing for Penny to do but stab at her own sliced turkey, so she drifted into the casual conversation Tippy started. She wasn't satisfied, she was even a little annoyed, for in these last few months Tippy had developed an amazing way of settling her own affairs. My goodness, Penny thought, when I was her age I leaned on David like a busted woodshed on the barn. And he wasn't even as much older than I was, as I'm older than she is.

It was very confusing. No one who looked as young and cute as Tippy should be so self-reliant. Her slender little neck rising out of its white collar didn't look strong enough to hold her round chin at such a determined angle, and all of her in the padded chair looked so small and feminine that Penny found herself asking suddenly, "Are you as tall as I am?"

"Yep. I'm five feet five," Tippy answered, laughing because Penny's thoughts were never where one expected them to be. "Why?"

"I haven't the least idea, except you look so little and I'd like to shake you. You won't even read the part?"

"I told you no, Pen." Tippy laid her spoon beside a glass that had held ice cream, and said with a pleased sigh, "I feel better inside. You must lunch with me next week."

"You can't afford it."

"Oh, not here. In the automat. And now, unhappy thought, I must go back to work. I'll see you Sunday if not before."

The luncheon was over. Work awaited her, and Tippy lost little time in getting back to it. She gave Penny a hasty kiss as she crawled backward out of a taxi, and went rushing through the lobby of her building and into an elevator that made its first stop at the twentieth floor. It occurred to her that thousands of girls in New York would fight and scramble for the part she had just turned down, that only one would be lucky or talented enough to land it, and while she rode up to her own unimportant little job, she decided to put in a word for one or two who were accepting television as a doorstep to Broadway.

The vast room of Studio One looked like an animated cartoon. Men were pushing great dollies into place, swinging the cameras they held into focus, flapping cables, muttering over lights that wouldn't work, and shouting at one another. The whole thing looked too jumbled ever to pull together, but Tippy knew it would. At one minute of three all the noise would cease. Actors would freeze in their places, the announcer would clear his throat, grasp his box of Crackle Snacks and be ready for his minute of selling time. A red light would show on one of the cameras before it began to grind, and Tippy would sit up straighter in the audition room, looking down through the glass panel, her notebook on her knee. It happened five days out of every week. Eight minutes of advertising and seven minutes of story went out all over the country, making women leave their work to cry over other peoples' trials and tribulations and write that *A Lantern of Love* was the finest program on the air.

Tippy's part was done. She had only to sit in her glass

case, and then repack the boxes of props and receive a new list of duties for tomorrow. As she wound her way through the confusion to check her return with Miss Turnbull, she thought her great-grandparents would have considered it a very peculiar way to earn a living.

CHAPTER II

TIPPY stood outside the little office in the parking lot and waited for her father to drive by and pick her up. They used the same small, convertible coupé David had given her for her trips back and forth to a junior college on the Hudson, and it provided comfortable transportation to work and a relaxing drive back to the country.

"Let's have the top down," she suggested, when it stopped beside her and her father leaned over to open the door. "I may have been hotter but I don't remember when."

Colonel Parrish pressed a button, and as the top swung back he remarked, "We'll probably have to come in on the bus a couple of days next week. We need new canvas."

"No, thanks. We'll borrow the family sedan from Mums."

25

Tippy leaned back comfortably and explained. "Mrs. Parrish doesn't work in a hot city, and she has a very nice daughter-in-law to ride her around if she's stuck without transportation. Carrol can send over any one of three cars. Oh, no," she said again, shaking back her hair and lifting her face to what little breeze there was between the high buildings, "you can't climb on and off of busses. Want me to drive."

"I'd rather do it. It takes the office kinks out of me."

Tippy turned to regard him. His hat lay on the seat beside him. His hair was almost silver-white. Pain wrinkles fanned out from his eyes that were as blue as David's and almost as brightly young, but his face, strong and finely molded, looked firmer and more alive than it had a year ago. "Work agrees with you, Dad," she said. "Did you settle all the world affairs for your public today?"

"Not exactly. You know," he flicked a glance at her and winked as he said, "I can't handle those Russians. Sometimes I'm glad I'm on radio instead of TV because I frown and make faces when I read some of the news bulletins. I can't even give my news analyses the old army slant and decide what the Communists are trying to do, or we either. But it's diverting. And your job?"

"Fun."

Tippy turned sideways on the seat and began to tell him about Penny's offer. They went up a ramp and onto the highway beside the Hudson River, and were across the George Washington Bridge before it was fully discussed to their satisfaction. And they were almost home before the rest of their day had been disposed of.

26

The great gates and lodge of Gladstone flashed by. David lived in there with his beautiful wife who had such a lot of money, and his two little boys. David had turned the estate into a paying farm, and both Tippy and her father stopped their conversation to see if they could find him anywhere in the broad, rolling fields.

His tractors were idle, far, far away, almost at the woods that rose like a green backdrop, so they went on past the road leading to Penny's quaint, rambling house that was very old and was called Round Tree Farm, although it had only six acres of ground. Just around a bend would be their own dear home, white and low and precious.

"Coming home's the loveliest part of the day," Tippy said, when they turned between two white gateposts and along the short driveway. "Hi, Switzy."

A small French poodle scampered like a prancing ink spot to meet them, and her voice was drowned by his frantic yelps of joy. "Down! Down!" she cried, jumping out before the car was fully braked in front of a white door and flagstone steps, hoping to save both him and the car's paint he was scratching as he leaped. "You idiot, you know I always come back."

Switzy didn't know, or if he did, he had to tell her how joyous he was; so she bent down and let him cover her face with kisses. It made him happy and it was what Ken had told him to do. "You take care of her, Switz, old boy," Ken had said, when he had bought her the tiny puppy in Switzerland and she had named him for his native land. Switzy had tried to do it through long, difficult months, and he saw no reason for her to go away and share her days with other people, now that she was happier again. She was enough for him, and he thought he should be enough for her. So he wept and barked over the anguish of their lost hours together, until she had to scold, laughingly, "Now that's enough. You couldn't have suffered all that in one day."

But he had. He sent the Oriental rug in the hall skidding, and ran back and forth along the long gray carpet in the living room. He snatched his ball from under the grand piano and flung it away. He bounced onto the wide seat in the front bay window and almost went out through leaded panes, and he caught his feet in lamp cords and fell over the wood basket by the fireplace. He went around in such excited circles that only the sound of Mrs. Parrish running down the stairs sent him dancing out to the hall again. "Yip, Yip," he barked. "She's home."

But Mrs. Parrish went to her husband. His face was the one she kissed first. And her brown eyes, so like Penny's, studied it for any sign of weariness, as she said, "Carrol was on the telephone and I couldn't get down in time to meet you."

"Is everything all right at Gladstone?"

"Fine. David bought Davy a larger pony today and turned the little one over to Langdon, and I've had Penny's two all afternoon. I've had a wonderful day, have you?"

This was their happy hour together. It always had been, as long as Tippy could remember. Once four children had shared it, then two had married, and Bobby, the noisy, the busy, the teasing one, had transferred his activities to a military academy that had managed to make him as sensible as he had been silly, and she was the only one who was left to see how deeply and dearly her parents loved each other.

They were on the divan now, the brown head and the silver close together, chattering away like two kids on a date, so she took her own black friend and sauntered out to the kitchen. "Good evening, Trudy, my pet," she said, opening a swinging door from the dining room to a serving pantry, and crossing waxed linoleum to hug a busy little person at the sink. "Did you miss me?"

"Law, Tippy, child." Trudy reached up to wipe her brown hands on a paper towel, and answered with her small, dark face beaming, "I knowed you was home. It don't matter how lonesome your mama and I get for you, Switzy gets lonesomer. Seems like, with this big yard and a brook out in back, he could find something to amuse hisself. Shame on you, Switzy," she scolded. But the little dog only sat down and grinned at her, his hot pink tongue hanging out. What little love he had left over from Tippy he gave her.

He watched Tippy sit down at the kitchen table by a window, pull a loaf of Trudy's fresh-baked bread toward her and begin to slice it. He could relax now; so he flopped over on his side and waited patiently for twilight and fireflies, for pleasant splashing with Tippy, through shallow water and over mossy stones.

Tippy finished the bread and began taking down plates and cups and saucers. Trudy had helped rear four little Parrishes and her bent back tired easily now. There were streaks of gray in her black hair, and her hands, so often clasped over her white apron while she delivered bits of sage advice, were gnarled with arthritis.

"I s'pose you'll be havin' a date tonight," she observed, "seein' as how your mama had to hump up the cleaners to bring your green dress back."

"Yep. Dr. White's nice son who works in the village chain store during college vacation has asked me to go stepping. He's very nice," she repeated.

"He is?" Trudy took a pair of bone-rimmed spectacles from her capacious apron pocket, put them on and regarded Tippy over their top. The spectacles were quite new and the whole Parrish family wondered why she wore them, since the prescription was mild and she rarely looked through the glass. "They help me see," she always said in answer to their curious queries. "Seems like I get a better view of a potato when I'm peelin' it, and when I look at somebody over 'em, they kind of blot out the rest of the room." So she regarded Tippy and asked, "Do you have fun on all these dates you go on, child?"

"Of course." Tippy stacked her china on a tray and said, "I wouldn't go out if I didn't."

"But you ain't serious about none of these boys, is you?"

"Um—no. I'm not serious about anyone, and you know it."

Tippy took place mats from a drawer, tucked them under her arm and would have picked up her tray, but Trudy laid a hand over hers.

"Child," she said, "I know you heart's still yearnin' for Mr. Ken. It keeps rememberin' the good times you had together, and it won't let you really look at anybody else. You

30

ain't *seein'* these boys, Tippy. You ain't even seein' Mr. Peter."

"I haven't had a chance to." Tippy laughed and tried to keep the conversation light. "Peter hasn't seen me—not since he graduated from the Point a year ago last June. As soon as he became Lieutenant Jordon, he gave me one month of his summer's leave, then away he went. How *could* I see him?"

"In his letters. The same way you still sees Mr. Ken, in your heart. He'll be comin' back one of these days and you won't even recognize him."

"Not recognize Peter? Oh, Trudy, don't be silly. I grew up with him." Tippy knew what Trudy was trying to tell her from her own deep wisdom, but she willfully chose to misunderstand. "I'd know Peter anywhere," she said. "He has nice yellow hair that he usually cuts too short, and gray eyes and a long chin, and he's almost as tall and stringy as Bobby. There."

"You ain't mentioned what's behind those gray eyes," Trudy persisted. "Or how straight he carries hisself so he can look out over the heads of little people, or that his chin needs to be kind of long to hold a good big mouth that likes to grin a lot. Those are the things you ain't seein'."

"Oh, pooh." Tippy forgot her tray and leaned over with both hands on the table to scowl at Trudy. "You are a busybody," she said with loving distinctness. "You know darn well I think about Peter. But what good is it to think about someone who's clear out in Texas? Just answer me that."

"He might come home."

"Huh. He's having a grand time. He gets into tanks with a

lot of other men and goes bumping around, and from the way he writes, you'd think he's personally responsible for the American flag getting onto its pole in the morning and safely down at night. He's practically the whole *army*." Tippy hunched up her shoulders in a way that was supposed to impress Trudy, then gave up trying to sidetrack the discussion, and said honestly, "Oh, darn it, Trudy, men have jobs. Peter wants to see me, I know he does, but he can't jump on a plane in answer to one of my droopy letters. *I* would. I would have," she corrected, "before I started working. There wouldn't be any reason why I couldn't have. I understand things better now. Oh, I'm no career girl," she said with a deprecatory laugh. "It just makes me understand that men are busy, that's all. Even Ken didn't have time to find— to find dying so hard, because he was so busy."

"I sees what you mean, child. Your mama and I've been kind of wonderin' what's goin' on in your head lately, and it's good to know. You keep right on bein' busy."

"And don't either one of you think I've forgotten Peter, I like him fine."

Tippy picked up her tray and sailed into the dining room, ready to set the table at last. She did it carefully, with tall candlesticks and a bowl of zinnias in the center, then stole past the living room archway and up the stairs.

Along the hall was her bedroom, her own peaceful, quiet place. Yellow tufted spreads covered the mahogany beds, yellow drapes hung at the windows, the walls were papered in a pattern of green ivy on a white background. Her favorite quilted chair stood by a table with a lamp on it, and

Switzy, padding along behind her, settled into his basket with a contented sigh.

They liked this place. And Tippy, walking to her dressing table, forgot she had come upstairs to remove the grime of a day in town. Trudy's talk still lingered in her mind and she stood looking down at two photographs in leather frames. On the righthand side of the dresser, Ken's fine face looked back at her from above a uniform: blue eyes that always had a sleepy look because of a downward slant at the outer corners, brown hair that sprouted into a double cowlick, could she but see under the overseas cap that hid it, a half-smile, so tender it made her want to touch her lips to it. She studied the photograph for some time before she turned to the other one.

Peter was as she had described him to Trudy. He wasn't handsome in a standardized way. His face was too long. But he was lean and rugged, even in his football uniform. Hands on his hips, his helmet hanging from one, he grinned out at her, just as he had after his last game for West Point, when the crowd was mobbing him as the hero who had piled up most of the points against Navy.

He had looked for Tippy over that jumping, seething mass which bore him triumphantly off the field; and, finding her, shrieking madly with the rest, had shouted, "Meet me at the gate!" Looking down at the photograph, Tippy sighed. She hadn't been very kind to Peter that day, for her thoughts had been with Ken who was in Korea. Peter was just Peter, the best player on the team. He was Alice Jordon's brother, part of a foursome and a lot of fun, but a date was only a date to her then, and there might be a letter at home from Ken.

33

"I wasn't nice to you," she said aloud to his picture. "Not then, or even when you graduated. And you were always so dear and kind to me. You—you took care of me, Peter, when I was so wretched and unhappy after Ken was gone, and you asked so little for yourself. I wonder if I can ever make it up to you. I wonder if I'm ever going to try."

Peter smiled back as if he found her perfect, but she sighed and shook her head. "I suppose I'm going to marry you," she said. "I halfway told you I would—someday. I will if you still want me to when you come back, but it seems sort of an unfair thing to do. I like you so much, and I love you, too, but . . . oh, gosh, Peter, I don't know."

She heard her father call from downstairs, and ran a hasty brush through her hair as she answered, "Coming."

Trudy had stirred up memories, as Trudy had meant to do, and she vowed to answer Peter's last letter tonight. She even considered canceling her engagement with Lyman White to do it, then shook her head. In the muddled mood I'm in, she thought, I'm apt to say too much. Peter might misunderstand and might even manage to wangle a leave and be disappointed. Nope, Tippy, my girl, hold onto your hat. You're much better off running errands for Miss Turnbull.

"Coming right down, Dad," she called again. "Just as soon as I scrub up." And she rushed off for a hasty wash, leaving the two photographs looking into space.

CHAPTER III

TIPPY worked busily on at her job. It was the hottest August she could remember. It was so hot that newspapers boasted of records, and she came out of air-conditioned studios into the blazing heat of late afternoon feeling as wilted as the flower in her father's buttonhole.

Penny had let someone else take over her part in *A Month of Sundays* and retired to the peace of the country for a well-earned rest, so there were no more of what Tippy called her "stylish luncheons." She missed them. She missed a lot of things, even Bobby's cheerful whistle that had filled the house during July, and the plates of food he had consumed

35

each day, and the evening jaunts he had taken her on, when she could supply the necessary money.

She went up to West Point to see him sometimes, but she didn't enjoy the dances as much as she had when Peter was there. Peter had been a first classman, older, and with definite ideas on what he wanted to do with his life. Bobby and his crowd seemed so silly. By dint of hard work and belated application, he was, to the family's great relief, starting on his next to the last year; and while he was older than Tippy, she thought he blundered along with about as much dignity and sense of direction as a Newfoundland pup. "Even Switzy," so she had told him all summer, "is smarter than you are."

To this he was apt to retort, "Sez who?", usually with his mouth full. And then, after such profound retaliation, he would drag his lanky frame from whatever prone position it happened to recline in, and say, "Come on, Switz, ol' brother, let's take our dumb selves away from here."

Switzy usually went, for they never moved farther than the kitchen. There would be a brief forage, followed by contented grunts as they sagged down again, with a new supply of food. But Tippy missed him. She might fuss at him because his blue stare looked straight through her when she wanted his attention, and his big hands shoved her out of his way, or his feet stuck out of the swing to trip her, but she wished he were home.

He was a pretty good brother, she thought. Nothing to compare with David, of course, who according to legend, had been all things to Penny; but he was a lot better than

36

nothing, and she resolved to go call upon him in his great stone fortress. She would have, too, but something else occurred to divert her. Miss Turnbull fell and broke her leg.

Miss Turnbull was a chunky woman, given to rushing at things. With a hop to this side and a skip to that, it was no wonder she finally stepped on a light cable that rolled under her foot. She went down with a crash, and those who rushed to her assistance were more surprised to find her lying still and speechless than hurt. Her eyes were closed, her head had banged the floor with a solid whack; and Tippy, the first to reach her, thought wildly of concussions and a possible skull fracture.

But it was the other end of her that was injured. Moans began coming from her lips, and her eyes fluttered open. "What time is it?" she asked into the faces bending over her.

Like an old steam engine, she was trying to run on schedule, and when she made an effort to lift her head, Tippy pushed it gently back. "It's still early," she said. "You haven't been out but a minute. Lie still, Miss Turnbull."

It was quite evident that something was seriously wrong, for Miss Turnbull obediently did as she was told. It was the first time such a thing had happened since Tippy had known her. A stagehand silently pointed to her leg that lay in a grotesque position and Tippy almost fainted herself at the sight of the twisted thing. The whole studio went round and round and turned upside down, but she managed to say, "I think—we'd—better—call a doctor."

"Oh, pish." Miss Turnbull got herself up on to her elbows, then gave a groan and fell back again. "Howard," she said through tight lips, to a burly electrician who looked about to cry, "don't just stand there. Help me up. All you people go away. I want to get up."

The little knot of actors and cameramen stepped back out of her vision but Tippy dropped to her knees. "Miss Turnbull," she said in a soft but firm voice, "you'll have to stay still for a little while. A doctor's coming because—we think you've broken your leg."

"Nonsense. I couldn't have. I simply had a nasty fall, that's all." Matilda Turnbull lifted snapping black eyes to Tippy. They always had to look out from under a frowze of gray curls tinted to a purplish platinum and over a nose that was as thin and beaked as a hawk's, so they had a constant peering expression. Just now they were so filled with pain that Tippy wanted them to close again in blessed unconsciousness.

It was a long time before a doctor could be found on another floor and still longer before an ambulance came. Miss Turnbull rallied and gave orders. She gritted out directions between clenched teeth, and when she was finally lifted and borne away on a litter, she went like a wounded campaigner demanding to stay and command his men. Her last order was to Tippy, and it was a feeble but heroic, "Take charge."

Tippy started in. From second in command she had risen suddenly to first. The play which would begin at three o'clock, for the delight of televiewers, would carry the caption, *A Lantern of Love.* The producer's name would follow, then the director's, then in very small but important type, "*Scenery by Matilda Turnbull.*" It was up to Tippy to keep the smallest name unsullied.

There was really very little left to do, she thought. The walls of the set were up. As part of an army family, moving onto army posts on sudden notice, Tippy felt that walls were all one needed. She had seen furniture unloaded from a van, whisked in by soldiers, and set in place. Sometimes each piece had had to be uncrated before it could settle into its selected spot, but by nightfall a whole house was livable. Dishes were unpacked, rugs were down, beds were made, and the kitchen was a functioning organization. Here she had only two rooms to furnish. They only had three sides and part of the work was done. And she had charts and specifications to follow, too. It looked very simple to her, and as she started in to direct it, she thought what child's play this would seem to her mother.

"Mums would never break a leg over where a pot of geraniums should sit," she scoffed, slapping the geraniums down where her diagram indicated, "window sill, exact center," and bending down to measure the distance from a kitchen table to the stove with a yardstick, and calling over her shoulder, "Oil the hinges on that door to the living room, Pete, so it opens easily for Grandma Bascomb's wheel chair, and ask Mr. Teague to check his lamps again."

She wasn't flustered. It was fun. The only difference she could see about the whole affair was that she wasn't saying, "Yes, Miss Turnbull." "Right here, Miss Turnbull." "I took care of that, Miss Turnbull," every other second; and, instead of streaking for her notebook and sitting behind her glass wall at three o'clock, she had a place backstage in the wings.

Everything went smoothly. The hammering stopped as soon as it ever had. The actors had as much time to get the feel of a set they knew by heart, the announcer had even more time to joke about his Crackle Snacks, and no one was out of breath or mad.

Tippy wondered why so much fuss was made each day over setting a silly little stage. But when four o'clock came and the verdict on Miss Turnbull's broken bone was given to the higher office, she learned the reason.

"Miss Parrish," the studio director said, looking across his big desk at her, as she sat in a square box of leather club chair, much too big for her, "I feel that Miss Turnbull's absence will be a great responsibility for you."

Tippy knew she didn't fit the chair, since it was designed for a man and almost swallowed her, and she doubted if she fitted Mr. Osborn's idea of a scenic director, either. There were two ways to make him really see her. One was to sit forward on the very edge of her chair and attract his attention, and the other was to lean back and let him hunt for her a little. She leaned back and rested her curly top against the cool leather.

"I'd be very happy to fill in for Miss Turnbull," she said. "It seems unfair to engage someone to take her place for such a short time." And she added to herself, "Because the other person might do a better job." But she didn't say it. "We have all the diagrams, you know, and we're using this same set tomorrow," she went on instead, her voice cool and composed. "It won't be hard."

Mr. Osborn looked at his program director. Elmer Floyd

had been wanting a change for this show and for the two other small sets Miss Turnbull designed, just to stop the constant grumbling and complaints of the crew, so he waited for the lucky young man to take his cue.

But Mr. Floyd was smoothing back his neat brown hair and looking at Tippy. He had been looking at her for some time, entranced by the way two little dimples played hide and seek around the corners of her mouth, and wondering if her eyes could be called a golden-brown, or were nearer the color of really fine topazes. A surprised, "What is your opinion, Mr. Floyd?" brought him back with a jerk.

"Why—er...." He must be out of his mind. Tippy was too young to handle a kindergarten, let alone a hard-boiled crew of technicians, and here was his chance to replace old Turnbull. "We can get Celeste Du Barry," he said. "I saw her yesterday."

"Fine."

The matter was settled. Tippy was back in her number two spot, which made no difference to her and only gave her another boss, but poor Miss Turnbull was out. Loyalty to her commander in chief, memory of her pain-racked face, her twisted leg, that was an injury incurred in line of duty, sat Tippy up straight again and whisked the dimples out of sight.

"Please, Mr. Osborn," she said, "let me try it for a day or two. It isn't hard. I know I can do it, if Mr. Floyd will let me try." She turned her eyes that *were* the color of topazes straight on the discomfited program director, and added softly, "Please give me a chance. I'll work very hard."

Had she known what she was saying, she might have bitten back the words, for "I'll work very hard" was a sentence to fly back and hit her. It was a boomerang. It was also a masterpiece of understatement.

She had the job. She was supreme commander of the sets, without a rise in pay, of course, without prestige or thanks, and still burdened with Miss Turnbull, who had a telephone beside her bed.

She almost crawled to the parking lot the second evening, for Miss Turnbull's leg was nicely set and the anesthetic had worn off. "Honestly, Dad," she said wearily, pulling herself into the car, "I can't get time to do my work. She's on the phone every minute. She wanted me to come to the hospital tonight, and if it hadn't been Friday, I'd have had to go. She put it off till Sunday and says we'll go over everything at night, every night, all next week. I guess," she ended with a sigh, "I'll have to move into the little apartment Penny and Josh keep in town. I don't see any other way."

"Then quit the job. Unless you're planning a career and see this chance as a boost," he said, knowing she wasn't and didn't, "give it up. It isn't worth it."

"Oh, yes it is. I started it. The studio would have hired Celeste Du Barry if I hadn't spoken up, and poor old Turnbull never would have got back in. She won't now, if I don't hang on." And she looked up to ask, "How long does it take a broken leg to heal?"

"That depends," he answered. "You said it was a clean break, so she may get around in a cast, with crutches, in a few weeks."

His answer brought a groan from Tippy. "I'll push her to work in a wheel chair," she vowed. "I'll get her there some way if I have to build a ramp and borrow David's station wagon. Say, maybe I could at that. Can't you just see Perkins rolling her in?"

Perkins was the English butler who had been with David's wife from her childhood. At the very thought of him pushing a wheel chair in striped trousers and morning coat, they burst out laughing and some of the tiredness went out of Tippy. "Well, I'll think of something," she decided, and leaned back to enjoy the drive.

A week of setting up housekeeping and tearing it down again went past in monotonous fashion. Tippy wondered how work could be so dear to Miss Turnbull's heart when it meant poring over sketches every night, conferences after the studio's closing hours, and only enough sleep for strength to rise and go at it again. She wondered why anyone would want to forge ahead in business; and when Penny and her husband dropped in at their own one-room efficiency apartment to see her one evening, she flopped straight out on a divan and told them so.

"It all depends on your point of view, pet," Penny said, looking fondly around the little room that bore so many scars of her work, and Josh's. "I've always loved hours and hours of rehearsing, and working late and crawling out of bed to start over." She sat down on the arm of Josh's chair and asked confidently, "We like it, don't we?"

"Sometimes." Josh's homely face broke into a grin. He had fine level eyes under straight black brows that were his only really good feature, for the others were too craggy. "I can remember a few dust-ups," he said laconically, looking up at her, "when you wanted to stay home and be a mother."

"Not when I was Tippy's age. I was afire with ambition." Penny took his hand that found its way around her waist and held it in both of hers, as she asked, "Why don't you give up the rat race, Tip?"

"Why don't you all stop *asking* me that?" Tippy flopped over on her side and waved an indignant arm. "We weren't reared to give up," she cried. "I started this thing and I *can't* give up!"

"Then take it easy," Penny persisted. "Coast along."

"Do we *ever* coast in our family?" Tippy wanted to know. "Have you ever *seen* us coast?" And she said at Penny's head that had to shake a denial, "Mums always told us, 'Don't start what you can't finish'; and one time when I was making a doll dress and the thing wouldn't fit, I decided just to bunch it on the doll. Trudy took it away from me and straightened it out across her knee. She smoothed it all out and said—I never have forgotten it—'Don't pucker your seams, child. If you pucker seams, you'll pucker life.' It makes a lot of sense."

Josh had to laugh into her tenacious misery. "You're sewing yourself quite a seam," he said. He tried to remember what one did with a needle and thread, then experimented with the comparison by saying, "How about leaving the bastings to stitch up the ravelings and coming out to dinner with us?"

"Me? Hah!" Tippy jumped up and began running about

the room. "I've lost my brief case!" she cried. "Oh dear, I'm not the brief case type. I've left it at the studio."

"Here it is." Penny pushed a leather portfolio out with her foot, and Tippy snatched it.

"I remember now," she said with a relieved sigh. "I flopped down in that chair when I first came home. I couldn't walk any farther. Thanks for the invitation, but I have another date tonight."

"Miss Turnbull?"

"Yep."

"But you have to eat."

"Oh, I'll eat." Tippy set her brief case by the door to a small foyer, on the floor, under the light switch, where it would be the last thing she saw before she turned off the lamps, and said, coming back, "I'll grab a bite in a drugstore, then I'll hop a subway and ride farther uptown than I ever went before, and take a three-block crosstown walk. After that my date will begin. I won't get away until midnight."

"Tippy, I don't like that." Penny stood up from her chair arm and looked at her husband. "She shouldn't be running around New York at night, alone, should she, Josh?"

"No, she shouldn't. Do you really have to check with old Turnbull, Tip?"

"Well, she's home from the hospital," Tippy explained feeling like a stray cat to whom people suddenly offered unexpected affection and a bowl of milk. "She likes to have her mail and know how things are going, and boss me a little. I thought I had to go."

45

"You don't. You're managing her job and that's enough."

"I *don't?*" Tippy marched over and brought the brief case back. "How are you going to get me out of it?" She asked, still holding the hated thing.

"By telephoning. It's all right, Tip," Penny said. "You can go to Turnbull's a couple of nights a week if you think you should, but there's no sense in working all day and fiddling with her every evening. Go right after work. Have Dad drive you by there and wait for you. It won't kill him to sit for an hour or so."

"He suggested that," Tippy said in quick defense, happy to pitch the brief case onto the divan where she had been, "but I thought I was sort of a pinch hitter and ought to listen to the coach. I never learn anything I don't already know," she said, shaking her head. "All the scenes have been done a dozen times before, and the writers took out the new sequence they had planned to start and offered to hold it over till next month. We have a lot of families going," she explained e-laborately. "Sometimes Grandma Bascomb, who's meant to be the lantern of love, is the only familiar one who shows up at the studio for weeks. Why, even Dania . . . "

"Let's go to dinner." Penny saw Tippy was truly interested in the serial whose sets she assembled, and slipped a wink to Josh. "Change your dress," she said, turning back, "while I telephone your ogre. Scoot."

The small apartment gave little privacy, since its living room had beds concealed in its walls and a chest of drawers took up most of the foyer, but Tippy squeezed past the chest to take a dress from the closet and retire to the bathroom.

46

Penny and Josh had saved her. She could sleep in her own bed tomorrow night, or even tonight if she weren't too tired to make the long drive out to the country with them; and no matter how long and hard the days might be from here on, Miss Turnbull wouldn't bark for three or four more hours at the end of them.

"Pen," she called, smoothing a navy blue taffeta skirt into place over a ruffled petticoat that made it swing out in a truly feminine fashion that delighted her, "I'm not puckering a seam, am I, by deserting Miss Turnbull?"

"Of course not, cherub," Penny called back. "I explained things to her and she understands. She accepted it on the solid basis of health and extreme youth. She wants to guard your health so you can 'emerge victorious.'" Penny laughed and said in a low voice to Josh, "Those were her very words. Anyone as nutty as that *would* have a kid working herself to a frazzle. But she told me I'm a 'magnificent' actress. She didn't mention you."

"She never heard of me." Josh stretched out his legs and clasped his hands behind his head. "Don't you wish it were time for us to dig in here again and work?" he asked, looking at the burns on the desk, an ink spot on the rug, worn chairs.

"Not yet." Penny took the place Tippy had left on the divan and tucked a pillow behind her back. "I have other work to do, too. I'm a mother. And just listen, my friend," she said, pointing her finger at him, "if you don't think that isn't a never-ending seam to sew just try it."

"I'd pucker the job. Fathering's the kind of thing you do

47

with nails and a hammer." Josh heard Tippy turn off the bathroom light and got up to pull Penny to her feet. "Let's all be normal folks tonight," he said, kissing her. "Let's leave all our fine ideals at home and go backstage to see that comedian you think's so funny, and his new musical. Let's give the kid some fun."

CHAPTER IV

THE telephone rang shrilly. It was eight o'clock in the evening and Tippy lay across her bed, fully dressed, one brown-and-white pump hanging half off her foot. Her cheeks were flushed with sleep and she stretched out a groping hand. "Hello," she said, and yawned.

"Hi, Tip," Peter's voice rumbled cheerily. "What're you doing?"

"*Peter!*" Her eyes popped open and she cried, "Where are you?"

"Texas. Want to see me?"

Peter had planned this question for days. Should his request for leave be approved, he had considered every answer he might receive, from a direct "no," to a breathless "how soon?". But the one that came along the wire made no sense at all, for Tippy said:

"Miss Turnbull broke her leg."

49

"Who's she?"

"Why, she's. . . ." There was a muffled giggle, then Tippy said, "Of course I want to see you, you nut. Miss Turnbull's my boss and she broke her leg, so I'm first in command and working like a dog."

"First in command of what? You haven't joined the WACs have you?"

"No, but I'm holding the fort—carrying the guidon, you know, marching at the head of the troop."

"Well, pip-pip, stout fellow, carry on."

"I will, old sport."

It was fun talking like this to Peter, and Tippy wriggled her shoes off the rest of the way and rubbed her feet together; Then she pulled herself up on her elbows, flexed her knees, and let her legs wave back and forth. "How could I see you in Texas?" she asked.

"I might get leave and I might hop a plane tomorrow. I might land in New York and you and I might go down to Alcie's and see how the bride's getting along."

"She isn't a bride any more," Tippy informed him. "Your little sister's been married for over a year."

"She's a bride to me. I haven't seen her since I came out here and I have a yen to. I also have a yen," he sent a modest cough along to her, "to show you how beautiful I am with a Texas tan."

"Dear goodness. Well, I haven't any yen to show you how haggard I am after two weeks of being a big executive," she retorted. "Can't you wait a week, till Turnbull learns to use her crutches?"

"I might."

His voice was suddenly serious, and it stopped Tippy's foolishness and made her say, "I don't mean that, Peter. I want you to come, you know I do. I'd have more time to play next week, that's all. I wouldn't be 'so plumb wore out,' as Trudy says."

"Texas is mighty nice through the wintah," he drawled. "Lots of brides out heayh, lots of purty little working girls have given up their jobs to marry officers."

"Pee-ter." Tippy laughed but said with a little catch in her voice, "No proposals over the telephone, please. You come on as you've planned. I'll manage some way. Shall I meet you?"

"Nope. I don't know if I can hook a ride on an army plane or will have to come commercial. I'll give you a buzz."

"But you're coming?"

"You bet I am. I have my leave orders in my pocket— effective at twenty-four hundred tonight."

"Then why are we wasting money *talking?* If you get in during the day, just be patient. I'll finish work as early as I can, then we can play. Oh, Peter," she said softly, "I'm so happy. I'm so *happy!* How long can you stay?"

"Fourteen days. See you tomorrow night. Good-by."

There were a few unintelligible words tacked on the end that she couldn't catch. They sounded like "my precious dearest," but they couldn't have been. They didn't fit Peter. "Tippy, darling," or "honey," was the most romantic endearment he had ever used, so it was hardly likely he would suddenly burst out with two such fancy expletives, wasting them both at once. Tippy rolled over on her back and flung her hands over her head.

"Switzy," she said, feeling black wool pass under her fingers, "Peter's such a quiet, dependable guy. Do you suppose he *did* say what I thought he said? Oh, he couldn't. Not *Peter*." She laughed softly in the dusk while Switzy chewed a burr out of his wool. And she went on, "I don't see how the dickens I'll be able to get away long enough to go down to Alcie's, it's almost to Philadelphia. I wish I didn't have a job." She rolled over again and looked down. "Switzy, I don't like a job," she whispered.

She was up at dawn. She had a dress to press and pack. It was a golden-brown, *bouffant* creation made of thin raw silk and worn over a crinoline. The whole thing, with the little velvet cap to match, required a box almost as long as the seat of the car, for it mustn't wrinkle.

"What will you do with it, honey?" her mother asked, watching Tippy in the middle of the living-room floor, struggling with tissue paper.

"Oh, I'll use the girls' washroom," Tippy answered, "if Peter comes before I leave the studio. It he doesn't, I'll drag it home again and wait here. I have a hunch he'll show up around five, though." She slapped on the lid, pushed it down and watched it spring up again. "String—camera—action!" she cried, holding it until her mother passed over a ball of twine.

The dress hung in Miss Turnbull's closet, now Tippy's. The excuse for a hat perched on a shelf, beside a china tea set that Miss Turnbull used quite grandly when she had an afternoon guest whom she wanted to impress. Tippy sat at Miss Turnbull's desk, plowing frantically through a stack of papers. It was almost noon. A valuable list of props was lost, Peter hadn't called, she would miss her lunch if she couldn't find the paper and had to rewrite it. "To heck with being an executive," she mumbled, and bent to a bottom drawer.

That was when she saw her shoes. They were the ones with brown tips she had worn yesterday, very white and clean—but they should have been brown suède. "Oh, my soul," she cried, and slammed shut the drawer to stare at them. "I forgot to change before I left home. Oh, heavens to Betsy!" Home was thirty miles away.

No matter how much time it took she had to telephone. Sitting there, jiggling the hook, fretting at the slow connection, she thought her mother would never answer the repeated ringing. But at last she did.

"*My shoes!*" Tippy wailed. "I forgot my brown shoes and I can't go out with Peter in these. Call Penny and see if she's coming in. Or Josh might be, or Carrol. Do something quick and call me back—no, wait a minute." She whisked open the top drawer and saw her brown suède purse lying where it should be. "At least I haven't completely lost my mind," she said, to her mother's bewilderment. "It's just the shoes. Will you call me back?"

"As soon as I can. But Tippy. . . . " Mrs. Parrish tried to say that Josh had already gone in town and Penny had stopped by on her way to the village. She found herself saying it to dead air, so let the receiver fall back into place before she put in a call to her daughter-in-law.

Tippy was searching for her paper again. If I were Miss Turnbull, she thought, banging drawers, I could send *me* out after the shoes. Or I could go out during my lunch hour and buy a new pair. I haven't any me to send or any lunch hour. Oh, drat it!

The paper turned up in a wrong file, and she snatched it out and went tearing down the corridor. She wished she knew more girls at WRIP. One of them might have a suggestion or at least a feminine shoulder to cry on; but during her five months of apprenticeship, her lunch hour had usually come long after theirs, and for the last two weeks it hadn't come at all.

She knew a few, of course, but Penny would have known them all by now and would have a dozen pairs of brown pumps to try on. She would be sitting in the midst of a veritable shoe store. Tippy saw so many high brown heels clipping along on strangers that she began to count them. Everyone wore brown shoes today, it seemed, even to the girl in charge of the musical record library.

"Hi, Stephanie," she cried, bouncing in and trying to read her list. "We need three records today. *Rock of Ages* by that quartet, and—oh, here, you read them, I'm too nervous."

Stephanie Miller was a pretty, dark girl who managed her library with competent efficiency. She had never seen the equally capable Miss Parrish in such a frenzy, and she asked curiously as she took the list, "What's wrong? Is Turnbull back?"

"Oh, I wish she were!" Tippy took time to perch on the

edge of a chair and rub her hands over her knees. "I'd at least have an hour off then," she said.

One of the records was on a top shelf, and as she reached for it, Stephanie asked over her shoulder, "Has something happened?"

"Everything. I have the most important date of my life tonight, and I'm all fouled up." She watched Stephanie's print dress slide up as she reached high above her head and stood on the tips of her pretty kid pumps. "I —I didn't know it was such an important date," she said, almost to herself, "until just now. Working certainly hashes things up, doesn't it?"

"Sometimes it does, but I like it. I'm studying to be an actress, but this isn't bad and it pays for dramatic school. Here's one of your records."

Tippy took the flat disk and sat holding it while she waited for the other two. "Would you mind if I ask to have any calls for me transferred up here?" she asked. "I'm expecting one from Mums, and goodness only knows where I'll be from now on. It's pretty important."

"Sure. Anything special you want me to tell her if I can't find you?"

"No, just tell her not to worry if she can't send the package in. She's apt to want to bring it herself, so say I've made other arrangements and have everything under control. And thanks a lot."

Tippy took her records and went back to the floor below. She arranged for her call at the switchboard and took time to go to a storeroom. A box of leftovers was kept in there: hats and clothes from old plays, perhaps even shoes. There might be a brown pair. But there wasn't.

A pair of sad black sandals came out, but they were large and flat. There were plenty of gloves, had it been only gloves she had forgotten, and even a brown linen purse. She dumped everything back in a jumble and went up the winding stairs again, to check a set in one of the smaller studios where a woman commentator would interview an author. Nothing was needed there but the divan and chair which were already in place, and a coffee table to hold the author's latest novel. She moved the chair out a little and straightened a small rug under it. And at one o'clock, Stephanie found her hanging window curtains for *A Lantern of Love.*

"Hey," she said looking up at the ladder where Tippy perched. "Your mother called and we had quite a chat. Why didn't you tell me you needed a pair of shoes?"

"I don't know. I didn't think of it, I guess." Tippy looked down with an embarrassed grin, and watched Stephanie slide off a pump and hop on one foot for balance.

"Here, try this," she said, holding it up. "If it doesn't fit, I promised your mother I'd whip out and buy you a pair. Take it."

Tippy let her curtain fall and reached for the shoe. An electrician, down on his hands and knees, growled and said, "What do you think you're doin', coverin' me up?" but it didn't matter. Brown suède or brown kid, she had a shoe on her foot. "Bless me, it fits," she breathed.

"Then come on down, Cinderella, and try the other one," Stephanie called up. "And give me yours."

"I'll have to finish the window. I'm almost through but that. Can you wait?"

"Yes, if you aren't too long."

The studio paid well for the work its employees did. This was pointed out to each individual before he or she was engaged, and it expected loyal service in exchange. Tippy carefully fastened her curtain to its rod, while Stephanie stood at a heavy green door, opened just enough for her to keep a watchful eye on her record room.

"I'm through," Tippy said, climbing down in her mixed footwear. "I don't see how I can ever thank you enough. I'll be so careful of them."

"They aren't my best ones," Stephanie answered, wishing she had worn her other pair today. "Want to make a permanent switch now, so you won't forget again?"

"I suppose I'd better."

The shiny brown pumps were a little too tight. Instead of an A width which she always wore, she was incased in a double A that pinched. But she was glad Stephanie wouldn't be the one to suffer, and she said again, "Golly, I'm grateful. If Miss Turnbull ever comes back, will you have lunch with me someday?"

"I'd love to."

Stephanie went back along the corridor, wondering what kind of man Tippy could be meeting that this date should be so important. She hoped he would appear before she left, so she could poke her head out and have a glimpse of him.

And Tippy would have been surprised to hear her tell one

57

of the other girls, "You have Parrish all wrong. She's really a
swell gal. I just lent her a pair of shoes."

Time crawled by in Studio One. It was the kind of day
when everything went wrong. Actors were hot and harried,
and they snapped at people whom they considered their sub-
ordinates. Tippy came in that class, mostly because of her
youth and because she looked so soft and vulnerable that it
was like punching a fist at a pillow. Painless. The blow satisfied everyone but Tippy, but she rallied from each one as
best she could. Five o'clock was all she thought of. She kept
her mind on five o'clock. At five o'clock they would all go
wherever they lived and she would put on her fine clothes
and forget them. When the hands on her watch were in exact
position, Peter or no Peter, she would walk out of here. Perhaps, she told herself, she would never come back.

But at quarter to four, Mr. Floyd sent for her. He had
plans it seemed, *and* changes, *and* the new serial would have
to begin, with or without Miss Turnbull. The sponsor and
director wanted a conference at five-thirty. Would she please
make it. He didn't use a question mark at the end of his request, Tippy noted. He finished it off with a period.

Five-thirty! That meant she would be two floors above,
high up in Mr. Osborn's mahogany office where sponsors
were always taken. With the switchboard closed. With people who had just wives waiting for them, so wouldn't hurry.
Tippy said, "Yes, Mr. Floyd, I'll be there."

Now what to do? She closed Miss Turnbull's office door
and locked it. She used Miss Turnbull's fancy, mirrored

lavatory and her scented soap. It was four o'clock and she didn't care who could hear her splashing. And she took her time about dressing. She would be working after hours and doing double duty tomorrow, so this period should belong to her. Surely, she reasoned, pulling on sheer, fresh hose, a girl was entitled to a *piece* of her day. A little tiny piece of it. Enough, at least, to keep herself clean!

Her feet hurt and her head ached, and she refused to answer a summons on her door. When what little of herself she could see in the small patch of mirror looked quite fresh and presentable, she climbed up on Miss Turnbull's leather chair to inspect the rest. She thought she would pass. Peter might not notice the violet smudges under her eyes, and he certainly wouldn't know that her belt was fastened a notch tighter than it had been last week. At any rate, it was time for Mr. Floyd and his sponsor, so she would have to do.

She got down from the chair, smoothed the rippling folds of her skirt once more, and marched across to open the door.

"Well, blow me down," Peter said, and caught her, tight, in his arms.

"Oh, Peter!" Tippy reached up and let herself cling to him. The corridor was empty, but it wouldn't have mattered if the whole staff had come tramping by because it was so wonderful to feel somebody holding her up. And she let her cheek rest against his lapel until he said, "How about a kiss, huh?", and she lifted her face.

"How did you get in this funny place?" she asked, pulling back to look at him, feeling young and full of sparkle again.

"A girl at the switchboard was in a hurry to take off and she said 'Go down there and wait, she's staying late tonight,' so I did. I knocked but you didn't hear me."

"I heard you." Tippy nodded, remembering the face she had made at the door. "I just didn't know it was you. Oh, Peter," she said, "you do look as beautiful as you said you would."

"I'm a handsome cuss. By reversing all accepted standards, I could win first prize in a beauty show." His nice grin flashed down and he held her away to look at her. "Boy, oh, boy, you're something to see," he said, and hugged her so hard her little hat went off the back of her head. "I'm the proudest guy in New York. Where do we go from here?"

It was hard to tell him but she had to. She left her hands resting on the broad shoulders of his uniform and watched to see the eagerness fade out of his eyes, but it didn't. He went right on smiling and nodding. "Okay," he said. "I'll stick around. We've plenty of days."

Plenty of days! Tippy's own amber eyes suddenly sobered. Ken had said almost that. He had said "We have three days, cherub." And she had opened a door in a Washington hotel and found him standing there, just as Peter had been today. Both in uniform, both with their arms outstretched. Dear, patient Peter. It wasn't fair to him for the memory of Ken always to crowd in between. Tippy was afraid he might have sensed her faint withdrawal, for he stooped to pick up her little hat.

But up he came, his face as bland as before, and clapped it on her head. "Let's get going," he said quickly. "The sooner we start, childie, the sooner we'll be off on our own."

60

He marched her along the hall, arm in arm, their brown shoes keeping step together; and it wasn't until she was sitting in Mr. Osborn's office, looking at Mr. Floyd and apparently absorbing what he was saying, that she figured out why Peter had coined a new endearment of his own. It was to be something special when he spoke to her, just as Ken's "cherub" had been.

Dear Peter, Tippy thought, smiling at Mr. Floyd's remarks and nodding her head approvingly at the sponsor's answer. She must remember to ask him how he had happened on this one, and why no one ever chose a grown-up, dignified nickname for her. Cherub—childie. She wished she wouldn't always have to seem so young.

CHAPTER V

"AND SO," Peter said, when they sat over candles and flowers, having their dinner in a small, cool restaurant, "I called Alcie and said we'd be down in time for dinner tomorrow night."

"But, Peter, I can't." Up to this moment, their conversation had filled in the year they had been apart. Peter had shown snapshots of his barracks, his pet tank named Annabelle, the jeep he used and had christened Kitten, because it was so playful and bouncy, and Tippy had given a colorful résumé of her days at WRIP. Now she frowned at him and said, "I explained to you that I always see Miss Turnbull on Saturday. She and I made a sort of compromise to go over the week's work all in one fell swoop. I'd have to come back into town on Saturday morning."

"Hmm." Peter studied her speculatively, his eyes as somber as hers, then he grinned. "I don't think so," he said. "Sunday evening ought to work out fine for Miss Turnbull." He stopped, looked directly at her under his level brows and asked, "You know your job, don't you?"

"Well, of course I do," she flung back indignantly. "It isn't that I'm *incompetent!*"

"Then let Turnbull do some reading and ironing over the week end, or maybe she has some stuff that needs mending. Let her entertain herself. Listen, childie," he said, leaning toward her, "you sat in conference with the big guns. You took the orders, you're carrying them out. Why do you want to go running to Turnbull for advice?"

"I don't. And why do you keep calling me that ridiculous name?"

"Do you mind it?"

"I don't know." Tippy looked at her plate, then up again into his steady gaze. Whatever she said would hurt him, but they couldn't skirt the past forever, not for two whole weeks, so she leaned her elbows on the table and said forthrightly, "Is it because—Ken called me 'cherub', Peter?"

"Not exactly." He, too, preferred to face an ordeal and have it over. Ken was there between them, just as he had been for a year before his death, and afterward, and might always be. Once he had accepted it. When Ken was living, it was Tippy's happiness that counted. Ken was the one she had chosen, so Peter had jogged along in the well-worn rut of friend. He was still that to her, apparently, and while it might be hard, he had decided that if he ever climbed out and onto the high ground of her affections, he had to pull himself up and put

64

himself there. "I don't know why I call you that, Tip," he said. "It suits you, someway. You're pretty tall but you don't look it. You're pretty independent, too, but I never think of you that way. I looked after you so much, I guess, after Ken was gone, that I've called you that to myself ever since I've been in Texas. I worried about you, and I'd find myself groaning, 'Oh, childie, childie, take it easy.' Maybe I got it from Trudy calling you 'child'. Who knows? But I'll stop if you want me to—at least out loud."

"I don't." Tippy laughed and folded her hands on the table like a good little girl come to tea. "I'd be very happy to accept your invitation to visit Mr. and Mrs. Jonathan Drayton," she said. "We'll drive down in my little car and we won't come back until time for work on Monday morning. There. Does that satisfy you, Lieutenant?"

"That's the way I like to hear you talk. Now." Peter expected quite a lot from these next two weeks, and he cleared the deck for action by pushing back his dessert plate and folding his arms on the table. "I'm traveling light," he said, "so I'll check my gear out of my hotel tomorrow and pick you up at the office."

"But you're coming out to stay with us," she protested. "Mums would never forgive me if you didn't."

"We'll wait and see when we come back."

"But how will I get home tonight?"

Tippy's face was so blank with dismay that he had to laugh. "I'll take you, idiot," he said, "and catch a bus back to town. I want to hop off early in the morning and go down to the academy where we have Neal and Vance in a summer camp. I'd like to take a look at Susan's camp, too, if I have a chance. Though perhaps Alcie can drive me over later. Having little Jordons sprinkled around the country seems kind of odd."

"You'll take my car," Tippy told him. "I'll bring you in early in the morning and you can drive right on. The car just sits here all day, and Dad will be driving his in, too. I never heard you talk so crazy."

"I never had so much on my mind. With Dad overseas, Alcie and I are responsible for the kids, more or less. Gwenn's no help with the little ones, way out in California; and even though Jenifer has two in England, it still leaves Alcie to keep tabs on the rest." He gave a rueful grin and said, "Nine Jordons. Gee, we must have thrown army posts into fits. I don't see how Dad ever took it and kept his senses, poor guy, without a wife to help him."

"You were a wonderful family," Tippy protested, with a nostalgic longing for the old days on Governors Island sweeping over her. "You were better and more economically organized than the army. You *were* the army. I never go over to the Island since Alcie was married and you moved away." And she asked abruptly, "You *are* coming out home with me, aren't you?"

"Sure your folks won't mind?"

She picked up her purse for answer and rummaged through it. "There," she said, laying an envelope on the table, "is a note from Mums, written in her most flowing hostess handwriting. She urges you to come; she practically gets down on her knees and begs you, so you don't need to bother about reading it now. And here is my check for the parking lot, and right behind you is our waiter, so lets pay for our elegant meal and be on our way."

"Perhaps childie doesn't suit you after all," Peter said, reaching back into his hip pocket for his wallet. "Perhaps I'd better call you Miss Fix-it."

"Stephanie calls me Cinderella," Tippy laughed, and told him about her shoes. She knew Peter so well again. It was as if they had never been apart; and at the end of her story she said plaintively, "The darn pumps hurt. One of them's over there by you, so you'll have to shove it back to me or I can't get up. Thanks loads. Oh, *dear!*"

The slipper refused to go on. She twisted it back and forth and finally managed to wriggle her toes into it, while Peter laid down some bills and watched her with amusement. She had such a childish dignity, such a little girl look of consternation, that he finally said, "Oh, come on, Tip, carry the thing. No, wait a minute."

He knelt down, and it didn't bother him at all that several diners watched him. On the football field with the eyes of thousands on him, his one thought had been to crouch and receive the ball as it was snapped to him; so he squatted beside Tippy's chair and got her foot into its shoe. "There you are, chum," he said. "You can take 'em off in the car." And he looked up at her from his undignified position to tease, "I guess you are childie, after all."

"Thanks, prince," she patted the top of his blond head. "I'm one of the wicked stepsisters and not Cinderella," she laughed. "The slipper doesn't fit. If you'll move yourself,

67

I'll get up and we'll go. We have a long drive ahead of us."

"You don't want to go dancing?" Peter stood up and rubbed the shining silk of her sleeve between his thumb and forefinger. "That's an awfully pretty dress just to take back home," he said. "I'd be mighty proud, pardner, to show off the girl who's in it."

"We'll go next week. Tonight," Tippy picked up her purse and gloves, and said as she squeezed out of her chair and past him, "I'd rather ride along under the stars and talk. I really haven't talked with you for such a very long time."

"Suits me." His glad expression was so sincere that she knew it was what he really wanted, too; and as they rode along in a cab to the almost empty parking lot where her little car waited, they chatted idly and in complete accord.

Dear, companionable Peter, she thought for the hundredth time in the last few years, when he was comfortably bedded down in the little upstairs sitting room that had housed Bobby through the summer, and she could hear him talking with her father. Solid and predictable. As dependable and even running as an electric clock. She sighed a little and gently closed her door.

The visit with Alcie would be fun, she told herself, not only while lying awake in bed that night, but all the next day, too. The excitement would begin again and she would feel as she had when she was dressing for Peter's coming, quivering with anticipation, not just loving and tender toward him, as she felt now. She loved him so much, and yet—she had to face it—there were times when he was too good and understanding, when he seemed a little dull.

And the next afternoon, riding along beside him on the wide Turnpike through the late sunshine, with the top back and the cool air ruffling up her hair, she pushed farther back against the seat and let her eyes turn to study him. She was sure she knew exactly what he was thinking: how fine this new highway was, how good it had been to see his little brothers. Peter's thoughts were like that; they followed a pattern. At least, they always had. And when he said, "Tip, light me a cigarette, will you?" she fished a package out of a patch pocket on the old sports coat he wore.

"There you are," she said, holding up his lighter; and she couldn't resist adding, "You never used to smoke so much."

"I never used to do a lot of things I do now," he replied, taking a contented puff.

"What sort of things?"

"Wouldn't you like to know!"

The answer surprised her, as did the little face he made, the way he lifted his eyebrows and stuck out his lower lip. And she had to ask, "When you asked me for a cigarette, were you thinking about Neal and Vance?"

"In a roundabout way. I was glad I hadn't given in to their begging and taken them out of camp for this week end. That's *one* of the things I do now, that I wouldn't have done before I got in the army. I stick to the things *I* want to do. The kids yelled bloody murder, and do you know what Vance called me?"

"No. What?"

"He stamped his foot and yelled, 'You're a mean old

69

man!' How's that for gratitude after I'd just given him five bucks?'"

Tippy had to laugh. She was glad she had been right. He *had* been thinking of the boys, but it surprised her to find that his thoughts had been anything but tender. His voice was even gruff as he went on, "Darned if I want a whole batch of kids when I marry. Jenifer and I were doing all right after Mother died, till Dad married again. Alcie and Gwenn weren't so hard to accept because they weren't much younger than we were and came along with their mother. But twins and babies! And then Dad even had to rescue Donny, who's only a cousin. Do you see any gray in my hair?"

He bent his head, and Tippy smashed down, hard, on the waving stubble blowing up in the wind. "What else were you thinking?" she asked, holding him.

"Oh, I was wondering what funny little Alcie's doing. She's the cream of the crop, she and Jenifer. I hoped she wasn't going to a lot of fuss over us, and was about to ask you if you thought she was. Was I silent that long?" he pulled away from her to ask. "I'm getting a frightful habit of talking with myself."

"You never were exactly the chatty type," she retorted. "You used to sit and listen to Alcie and me, and never say a word."

"How could I? Sisters above me, sisters below me. How could one poor boy ever hope to put in a word? Why, I was the best trained brother in existence, and the most patient till I got my own bachelor quarters."

"Now you're a mean old man."

"With my own record changer that no one touches, and a good lamp, and a wicker chair that's comfortable but a little busted, and my good old mattress I bought when I left the Point. That mattress," he said, "has seen me through a lot, so I've sort of retired it to pasture, you might say, by not rolling it up in cadet fashion every morning. It just lies there on the bed all day, resting its poor, tired stuffing. I kind of like being a mean old man."

Tippy suddenly realized that Peter hadn't made any of his usual proposals of marriage. Not once, not all last night or today, had he urged her to marry him and go back to Texas. She blinked with surprise and felt a blush rising for the silly answer she had made to his remark on the telephone. He had spoken of the pretty brides in Texas and she had accepted it as a proposal. He must have thought she had snatched at it, for he liked his bachelor quarters and his life. Her cheeks were very pink and she was glad he had to watch the road until they cooled.

Even when she thought it safe to speak, so he could turn his head and not find her looking like the setting sun, she could think of no clever retort. She was too embarrassed, too surprised and bewildered. And she sat listening to him tell about the Chinese rug he had bought from an officer's wife, much too fine and fancy for the rest of his battered room, while she tried to think back and remember when *was* the last time he had spoken of marriage. She couldn't. It would take some research, some mulling through the bundle of his letters.

"No batch of kids," he had said. "My lamp, my chair, my mattress." Tippy found herself laughing inwardly, not at Peter, but at her own profound conceit. Predictable? Dependable? Not on your life! And she said aloud, "I think you *are* a mean old man."

CHAPTER VI

ALICE JORDON DRAYTON surveyed her castle and found it good—very, very good. And beautiful. In fact, it was about the most beautiful house any proud bride could display to her guests.

It was an old house, built sometime in the late seventeen hundreds, and it was as sturdy as fine beams and handmade brick and wide clapboards could make it. It was put together to last beyond all the generations who had already lived and died in it, and she thought how lucky she was to have it for her very own.

It was almost her own, for it belonged to Jonathan's sister, Christy. A crotchety old cousin had bought it from other relatives and given it to Christy; and since she was happily going to college, she didn't need it. Cousin Edgar, who was no longer in the land of the living, had even willed her his own and much finer home where her family now lived, so she was glad to let Jonathan pay a modest rent for this one.

73

Alice dusted and cleaned each morning, rejoicing in her good fortune and savoring, for the first time in her life, the feeling of permanence. Army families often live in old houses, ones where drains clog and repairs must be made, but, as she repeatedly pointed out to Jonathan, they never move into a real antique. Not the kind that has people stopping in the road to admire it.

She wanted to own it. Jonathan did, too, in a way; and they had spent many evenings before their open fire or wandering in their orchard, considering the magnificent daring of putting the money Alice had inherited from her mother into this one gigantic leap.

"You aren't twenty-one yet," he had pointed out sensibly, one lazy Sunday evening, when Alice was lying on her stomach before the fireplace, shaking a wire basket of popcorn over red coals. "Even if your father would agree to let you, it's a big undertaking."

Her brown head was almost russet in the firelight. She looked like a serious little girl. Straight brown hair hung about her face and curved gently in to hug her neck, and a straight brown bang cut cleanly across her forehead, just above her eyes that were large and deeply gray, and she waved bare legs that ended in moccasins. "I know all the arguments, darling," she returned, shaking harder as white kernals began bursting against the wire mesh. " 'How do we know we'll want to live here forever?' 'How do we know you won't be called up for service?' 'How do we know you're going to be a financial success?' We just know, that's all. Please hand me that bowl."

She swung around and rubbed her cheek against Jonathan's hair as he bent down to set a yellow bowl beside her. He was so big. He needed a big house with lots of room, for he was a blond Viking. He was going to do wonderful things; Alice knew it, and they were the two happiest people in the whole wide world. She was so happy it sometimes hurt. When she was alone and watching for him to come home, there would be an ecstatic pain in her chest that cut off her breathing. Her heart skipped beats and bounced. It always happened at the sound of a car far down the road, and it always ended in a burst of skyrockets when the car turned in and stopped beside the house.

Alice enjoyed the misery, the bumping and thumping, the suspense of watching for just the right car; and on the evening of her telephone call from Peter, she went streaking across the grass, hitting every other flagstone. She wore a plastic apron over her shorts, and it slapped against her legs as she ran.

"Oh, Jon," she cried, as he caught her around the waist and swung her up, "Peter's coming! He and Tippy. Oh, isn't it exciting?"

"Swell. Give me a kiss."

She clutched him around the neck and he let her hang as he started walking. "Wait," she panted, her toes not quite touching the ground. "Stop, you dope. I can't kiss you this way. Hold still!"

Jonathan bent back with her weight and only laughed. He marched on with her dangling, until they reached the step to the porch and she could contact something solid.

"Strong man," she taunted, unclasping her arms and pushing him away. "Smart guy, brute. Now I won't kiss you."

That started a chase through the house. The stairs creaked as she fled upward, and doors to decorous, old-fashioned bedrooms banged as she raced through. The polished banister offered a downward slide for freedom, and a potted plant shot off the coffee table as she used the back of a divan for a fort.

"I give up—I give up!" she cried, knowing he was about to catch her anyway; and she flopped limply over his arm.

"Fainted, huh?" he returned calmly, carrying her toward the kitchen. "A little cold water will fix you up. Nice cold water on your head will revive you."

"Jonathan Drayton, don't you dare!" Alice kicked in earnest. It was no use, so she gave up sweetly with her cheek pressed against his, one hand turning his lips to meet hers. "Oh, I do love you so much," she whispered, resting against him. And she lifted her head to ask, "We do have fun, don't we?"

"The rest of the day's just eyewash. Now," he questioned, setting her on her feet, "what about Peter? I've had some very coltish exercise after a bad day in town, so give me the dope. When's he coming?"

Alice began to explain again. "Tomorrow," she said, "just as soon as Tippy gets off from work. We have the badminton court to cut tonight, in case they want to play, and there's the kitchen floor to scrub and wax again, and all that stuff to move in the garage so Tippy's car can go in—I suppose they'll come in her car, since Peter flew to New York—

and you really should take your junk out of the closet Peter will use, and clean the basement."

"Hey, wait a minute." Jonathan thrust out his chin and glowered at her. "This is your brother coming, isn't it?"

"Sure."

"Then why not get some work out of *him?* He was my best man at our wedding and I've always wanted to get even for the way he fouled me up over the ring. What's wrong with having *him* mow and clean? And why not let Tippy do the kitchen floor?"

Alice considered the matter judicially. "All right," she said. "I've always wanted a butler and a maid. I don't think Tippy cooks as well as I do, though," she added, mischief in her upturned eyes. "But we can eat a lot tonight and starve quite comfortably over the week end."

They carried their evening meal out to the orchard and sat on the grass to eat it, and Jonathan picked two round yellow apples for their dessert. Afterward, he scoured the green linoleum in the kitchen while Alice sat on a stool and watched him. And when it shone with a patent leather polish, they went upstairs to hang a last pair of drapes in a guest room.

"They really look quite professional, don't they?" she said, smoothing the pink material of one she still held and proud of the pleats at its top.

"Custom made." Jonathan, reaching up, also smoothed and adjusted as she had taught him to do, and squinted underneath to see if the pins were properly hung through their rings. "Shoot me the next one, bride," he ordered.

"Here it is." She held the curtain out to him and wished she could stand on the floor and reach so high. It would save such a lot of climbing on and off of stools. "Do you suppose Peter might want some of the furniture?" she asked. "If he and Tippy decide to get married?"

The old house had five bedrooms, a living room and a newer addition of a library, that were partly filled with Jordon furniture. General Jordon had had it moved down when he was ordered overseas instead of putting it in storage, and for two young people who had no possessions of their own except their wedding gifts, it, with what the Draytons had left when they moved into their new, richly furnished home, made a splendid showing. "Part of it belongs to him," Alice said, "because some of it was his mother's. Jenifer wouldn't want any, being married to a lord and expecting to inherit a batch of castles someday, and Gwen wouldn't be caught dead with just regular furniture in Hollywood—she has to have the modern stuff—but I'll bet Peter can use some."

"Wait till he gets a wife." Jonathan stepped back to scrutinize his handiwork, and said practically, "Your father just lent it to us, you know. He'll probably have a house of his own again someday. We can't go stringing it around the country."

"No, but it might help Peter. I surely would like to help him," Alice sighed.

"He'll manage for himself." Jonathan hooked an arm through hers and said with her leaning against him, "He's a great guy. Why, the last time Christy was home she said she thought Tippy was nuts. She said. . . ."

78

"Jon!" Alice whirled him around and grabbed him by both arms. "That's it!" she cried. "Christy will simply have to come here for the week end. She can. No matter what plans she's made, she'll simply have to come over. Oh, you're wonderful to have thought of it!"

"What did I think of?" Unaccustomed to worrying over anyone's love affairs but his own, his mind had traveled more slowly than hers, and he had to have her plot in detail:

"Why Christy can make Tip jealous. She can make a play for Peter that will knock Tip for a loop."

"But how do you know she'll want to? That doesn't sound like Chris."

"Oh, she will, she'll have to. I'd thought of Maxsie Green, that girl Peter went around with while Tippy was in Germany, but she isn't the type to even let Tippy stick around and compete."

"And you think Chris will?"

"Of course! She can't see anyone but Roger Lynn, anyway, and she has dozens of men of her own. I think I'll invite Roger too. Let's make it a house party, huh?"

She looked up at him with her little face so eager, her big gray eyes so shining, that Jonathan lost all interest in Peter or anything else. "Oh, Alcie, darling," he said softly, "I don't care what happens to anyone else in the world, because I have you. Invite all the gals for Peter you want but you stick close to me."

"You notice I haven't suggested anyone who'll give me competition, don't you?" she teased in return. "Not me. Little Alcie Jordon was never one to take a chance. Let's go telephone Christy. And let's plan a big party for Saturday night, with lots of people."

"Perhaps we shouldn't keep Chris right in the house," he said, finally catching the spirit of the thing, and planning with her. "I'd just let her pop in and out, if I were you, sort of unexpectedly. She's good at that. Whenever Pete and Tippy get bogged down in a twosome, or maybe having a pretty good time, in will come Miss Christy Drayton, with a lot of new ideas for fun."

"And off goes Peter. Wonderful! And Roger stays over at his house, too, and doesn't clutter up the scene as a relief man. Oh, Jon," she cried, "how did I ever manage when I didn't have you to fix things for me?"

"Darned if I know," he answered. "Are you going to alert Chris if we do it my way?"

"I'll have to alert her or she might go off. And we have to plan the party. Tomorrow night we'll all stay home—with Chris around—and Sunday we might go on a picnic or something. I won't worry about that part yet. Let's go call Christy."

Alice sat hunched over the telephone so long that Jonathan became impatient. It was all right while she giggled and explained what she wanted Christy to do in the interest of furthering romance, but he couldn't see what "that simply darling little suit" had to do with it. Christy had found the suit in a "darling little Philadelphia shop," for college, and from Alice's ecstatic repetition of its color, trim, and style, he could have walked into the store and picked it off a rack. And then there was a "little hat" and shoes, and a movie they had missed. All in all, by the time Alice let the telephone wire rest again, he had forgotten the outcome of the original question; but she remembered.

"Christy says okay," she informed him, hanging over the back of his chair and pushing aside the magazine he hadn't been able to concentrate on. "She's been buying her clothes for college," she told him.

"So I heard. She has to return the black kid shoes and her hat has a thingamabob in front. What is a thingamabob?"

"It's the same as a thingamajigger." Alice rested her chin on the top of his head and said dreamily, "I remember when I went to college. I only lasted one year because you came along. I had a new fur coat and a green suit and a hat with a long feather. . . ."

"A thingamabob."

"Oh, a beautiful thingamabob, sticking right straight out. It jabbed everybody in the eye and Daddy said it was a hazard. Now Christy's going to be a junior, while I—oh dear, I'm nothing but a—housewife."

"Sorry?"

"Not a bit. But you know what I did?" she leaned around until she could look at him. "A census man came here the other day, and when he asked me what my occupation was, I said, 'I'm a *home executive*.' I am. I think 'housewife' is inadequate. Running a home, not just a house, takes execution. And management, and a lot of brains."

"You have something there. I like the term better, myself. Remember the guy on TV we heard the other night? He said he didn't see why women don't think up a better name for their work. You can't be a husband's wife and a house's wife at the same time. So you just be my wife."

"Forever and ever. Would you like to help me make up the beds in the guest rooms?"

"Uh!" Jonathan gave a groan but stood up. "I'll do it on one condition," he said.

"What's that?"

"That you won't spend any more evenings with Christy."

"Why, you great big hunk of jealousy!" she cried. "Jealous of your own little sister!"

She still leaned over the chair back with her hands clasped, and he swung around with a "Boo!" that sent her flying. "I'll give you three before I start," he shouted after her. "If you aren't on the top step before I am. . . ." He stopped and grinned, because Alice's flat soles were already smacking against the polished treads.

CHAPTER VII

"LET's announce ourselves," Tippy said, when they were on a cross-country road and could see a green roof through the trees. "Keep whacking the horn."

She reached over, and together they pushed down a chrome ring on the steering wheel until the air was filled with a squawking din. It brought two figures in shorts up from the cool front step and made the smallest one smooth its hair and ask, "Do I have any lipstick on?"

"Enough. I hope I haven't." The big one brought out a clean white handkerchief and scrubbed hurriedly, then used the handkerchief for a flag of welcome as the car turned in.

"Peter!" Alice cried, and went dancing across the grass. "Hi, Peter. Hi, Tippy, too, but mostly Peter. Oh, *please* get out so I can hug you!"

83

"Coming. Gosh, it's good!"

Peter slid out of the car and Tippy tried to see what sort of kiss he gave Alice. It was, so far as she could tell, much like the one she had received. It might not have lasted as long, but it was as thorough, and the hug that followed it gave Jonathan time to help her out of the car and say, with his arm around her shoulders, "Thought you were never coming down again, Tip. We haven't seen you for months. Hi, Pete, you old Texan!"

"I never knew it would feel so good to get home," Peter said, pumping Jonathan's hand and hanging onto Alice, "Lordy, lordy!"

"You'll think you're really home," Alice chattered happily, "when you come inside and see all the old familiar furniture. I told Jon last night that I think you ought to have some of it. Maybe not the grand piano or the heavy pieces, but at least your bedroom set and your own mother's silver tea service."

"Me?" Peter laughed and hugged her again. "What would I do with furniture?" he asked; and Tippy felt her silly flush bloom again as he added, "Bachelors have to travel light."

"Well, come on in and see the works." Jonathan led the way with Peter's floppy canvas bag and Tippy's case.

He was always proud of the fine old house and the way it welcomed guests, so comfortably gracious, and he stopped in the narrow, shining hall with a glad air of ownership. "It's ours," he said, before going on up the stairs with the luggage, "but Alcie's the gal who made it. How about getting out of your store clothes and into country stuff?"

84

"Yea, man, as soon as I look around a little. I haven't been here since you added the Jordon touch." Peter walked slowly about the big, square living room. "What do you know!" he said. "Here's that lamp we all chipped in and gave Dad for Christmas, when he wanted a golf bag. And here's the scar Gwen burned on the table when she was fiddling with pyrography, and the little embroidered footstool Mother made. She was a wonderful woman, Alcie, that mother of yours."

He stood looking down at bright embroidered roses, and Alice went across the room to tuck her arm through his. "Does it make you homesick, Peter?" she asked.

"Sort of. We're all so scattered now. It makes me want to go back and do it all over." Then he shook his head and said, "Gosh, I don't know why. I can remember one night—I guess I must have been about fourteen—of thinking, Heck, what's the use? I'd had you kids in my hair all day, especially Gwen, and I sat out in the dark and considered running away. I didn't think anyone would even miss me. Then you came out and sat down on the bench beside me—remember that bench down in Florida? You sat down and put a cold little paw in mine. We just sat there. You were such an understanding little kid, Alcie."

"The bench had 'A. Cadwallader, Staple and Fancy Groceries' on it," she laughed; and Peter's retrospective loneliness was broken.

"In great big letters," he said. "Hi, there, Tip, where did you come from?"

"Out of the past with you," she answered. "I know

85

exactly what you're feeling, because I never come down here that I don't get homesick for Governors Island and the way we used to go in gangs to the movies, and squabble over tennis and ride around behind Royal, in that high old surrey you used to have. I know just how homesick it makes you," she repeated with a sigh.

"Well, I guess we have to grow up." Peter slipped off his coat and said with it draped over his arm, "Cool as you keep it in here, Mrs. Drayton, it's hot. It won't take me a minute to change. Come on, Tip. 'Mrs. Drayton' has a mighty funny sound, hasn't it? I'd rather have kept her little Alcie Jordon."

"Where?"

"Huh?"

"I mean where would you have kept her?" she said as they went up the stairs together. "Your father's in Turkey, and the rest of you all went off about your own affairs. I can't see that it would have been any great shakes for Alcie to have parked somewhere and taken care of the little kids. Alice Jordon Drayton sounds like a good solution to me."

"Well, aren't we haughty!" Peter turned off at a room whose furniture he recognized. He started to close the door, then leaned out around the casing and shouted, "Last one down is a ring-tailed monkey!"

That had been a challenge since the time of Penny's young crowd, and Tippy put on a burst of speed. Bang went her door as she jerked off her print dress and kicked off her shoes. The locks on her case stuck and she couldn't find her white shorts without tossing everything on the bed. Her socks weren't in any of the pockets, and she managed to button a red-and-white checked blouse while she pawed through the mass of lingerie and summer dresses with her free hand. Finally she snatched a pair of red loafers and dashed back along the hall, barefooted, and gloating over the racket still going on behind Peter's door.

"You're a ring-tailed monkey!" she shouted, as he thumped the stairs behind her; and it was only by spreading out her arms and leaping the last two steps that she managed to hold him back and skid into the living room ahead of him.

"That's not fair," he protested, looking as disheveled as she did. "I took time to put on my sneakers."

"But your shirt's buttoned up all crooked and the tail's hanging out."

"I wear it that way." He looked down at the peculiar front of his shirt, redid a button or two, and left the rest flapping. "Cooler this way. Okay," he gave in. "What's the forfeit?"

Tippy considered. It had been so long since they had played the game that she had to decide what would make Peter suffer most. "I guess you'll have to do my share of the dishes," she pronounced tentatively. "No, Alcie won't want you breaking her good china, so perhaps you'd better make the beds."

"That's easy. I learned to make a very military bed at the Point, and I always made 'em at home."

"Then I'll think of something else. The fine is delayed," she said, "until I want to collect it. Well, for goodness' sakes, where did Alcie and Jon go?"

The living room was empty. The kitchen was, too, when they wandered out there, although they could see that someone had made recent preparations for dinner. A pot boiled on the stove and an enticing aroma came from the oven.

"Let's take a look around," Peter suggested, looking out through a screen door that opened above a stone, time-worn step. "Although, I think," he turned back to whisper dramatically, "they are trying to leave us—alone."

"Why?"

"Romance, pal. In their romantic minds nothing jingles but happy wedding bells. Didn't you hear Alcie offer me furniture? Can't you just hear her saying, 'Now, Jon, give them time to discuss it. At *least* give him time to kiss her in privacy.' "

"Do you want to kiss me?"

Tippy stood by the door, too, and she looked up with teasing eyes that held a serious question behind them, but he only answered lightly, "Sure, you're very kissable."

"I'll take that for my forfeit. Delayed," she said hastily, "and *on demand*. Okay?"

"Okay."

He held open the screen door and she slipped past him, a little hurt, a little disappointed. Why, she didn't know, for he promptly sat down on the cool step and patted her bare toes.

"Gosh, childie," he said, "can't you ever put on your own shoes? Lift up your foot." And after he had her sturdily shod in her red moccasins, he held her hand tightly as they went around the house together.

Alice and Jonathan were far out on the side lawn under a giant oak tree. Jonathan had a folded green-and-white lawn umbrella over his shoulder and Alice was dusting off a white table while a pretty girl sat on a cushioned chaisette and watched her.

"Bless my soul, that must be Christy," Peter said. "Well, what do you know. Except for a name in Alcie's letters, I'd forgotten the kid. She looks kind of cute from here."

"She is." Tippy matched her steps to his as they reached farther out, and reasoned with herself. "Naturally men like to see a lot of pretty girls," she told her foolish pride because he walked so fast. "I can't expect him to look at just me all the time—especially when I'm not so much of a muchness."

Christy held a glass dish on her lap, and she set it on the table to reach up and greet Peter. She was pretty, prettier than Tippy had ever seen her, for college had given her a careless dignity. Her gray eyes were unusually wide-spaced. They were so far apart above her straight little nose that they gave her face a look of inquiring eagerness, and her teeth flashed white through a deep, summer tan. Tennis and swimming had browned her, until Tippy, comparing the arms reaching up to Peter with the ones that had carried props for Miss Turnbull all summer, felt like an anemic specimen of maidenhood.

"Hello, there, sort of brother-in-law," Christy said, giving Peter's hands a good firm shake. "I'm glad to see you again."

"And how you've changed. Wow!" Peter expressed frank admiration. He forgot to let go of her hands until she took them away, then he sat down on the chaisette beside her.

"Mother sent us a deep-dish apple pie," Alice said, gleeful and pleased with the way her actors were playing their parts. Christy knew her lines but Peter didn't. He was simply snapping up cues and having a lovely time. Tippy looked like a puzzled extra who had wandered in by mistake. So Alice walked over and let her smell the pie. "Good! Hm?" she said, and in the same breath asked Christy, "You're staying to dinner, aren't you, Chris?"

"Thanks, but I can't. Roger's coming to our house. I just came over to bring your dessert."

She stood up, and Alice was satisfied. A little dose of Christy was enough for the moment, and her small face looked so completely pleased that Jonathan ventured a pinch on the compact seat of her shorts.

"Stop gloating," he warned, under cover of Peter walking Christy back to her car and Tippy carrying the pie in a lonesome march to the kitchen. "It'd be a fine thing if he should transfer his affections to Chris, when she doesn't want him. You're apt to land in trouble yet."

"No, I won't." Alice was so proud of her machinations that she hugged herself. "I know Peter and I know Christy, and, I hope, to goodness' sake, that I know Tippy. She simply has to stop remembering Ken, Jon, and measuring everything by a lost love. He was a nice guy, but she can't have him," she said, suddenly serious. "Peter's a nice guy, too. I've known them both; and, of the two, I think he's even finer. I want him happy. And if Tippy doesn't fall for him, Christy might. She might, mightn't she?" she asked, looking up.

"Darned if I know, but I'm getting hungry."

Jonathan was happily married, so let the others take care of themselves. "Nobody helped me," he said aloud. "I had to beat out Bobby Parrish, all by myself. I had to camp on your doorstep and beg for dates and sell myself."

"Which you did—with all your worldly goods. And, I might add, I bought a very good bargain. Now I'll feed you."

Dinner, around the white table, with hurricane lamps to break the late twilight, was fun. Alice's roast came out of the oven, crusty brown on the outside, a succulent rare pink within, and a heap of corn on a platter went down, down, down, until only one ear was left. The apple pie came back. Tippy brought it on a tray with plates and forks, and Peter sprang up to help her.

Fireflies studded the night like dancing stars and the air was cooled by the lazily waving leaves of the trees.

"This is the way to live," Peter said, setting his plate on the tray and stretching out on the grass. "Nothing like it. Peace and serenity at the end of the day. Funny though," he went on, lighting a cigarette and blowing out a lazy swirl of smoke, "I'd rather have the army. I'd rather bang around in a tank on a hot terrain or fuss over a lot of paper work in a boiling, temporary shack, and come back to Fort Bliss in the evening."

" 'There's something about a soldier,' " Alice chanted. " 'There's something about a soldier that is grand, grand, grand.' "

The others took up the song with her until Peter said, "I guess that's it. When I drive up at night and Rollo wags his tail and tells me how many kids he's chased on the officers' line, and that the prison detail mowed the patch of ground around our wooden B.O.Q., and that retreat was a minute late because the gun wouldn't fire, I say to myself, 'Boy, you're home.' Rollo sent his regards to you, by the way."

Tippy remembered the gray mass of hair that always chose the best chair on the Jordon porch. Two beady eyes and a red tongue seemed to be all the face it had, and she asked, "Does he like it out there?"

"I guess he has to. He's not as high ranking as he used to be when he was a general's dog, but he makes out. He's good company on the nights I'm home."

"What do you do in the evenings?" Tippy cleared her throat at the end of the sentence because her voice sounded feeble, as if it had been pushed out.

"Oh, I go to a movie sometimes," he answered easily, "or drive into El Paso. I eat a lot of my meals at the club and something usually turns up. Lots of nights Rollo and I stay home and read."

No girls. Tippy wanted to ask about a few, but Alice was saying, "We thought we'd have a crowd in tomorrow night, sort of a party. Jon has to work till noon, but after that he's free."

"Think I could beat you at tennis?" Jonathan asked. "We can go over to the folks and play, or we can have a rousing game of badminton here at home."

"Anything sounds good."

"And Sunday–Sunday I have a surprise! Oh, I do hope I won't give it away," Alice mumbled through Jonathan's hand over her mouth. "I won't, so you can let go of me. Honestly," she protested, "people never think I can keep a secret."

"Which you can't." Jonathan laughed and boosted her to her feet. "We have to do our homework," he whispered loudly, so the others would be sure to hear. "If Chris and Roger should come over, you'll sit around like a hostess and I'll end up in the kitchen, all by myself."

"You'd have me," Tippy said, and hated herself for giving it such a meowish sound, just because Christy might come back and interest Peter. And she corrected quickly, "I'd help you, Jon, quick, like a flash. We all would."

"Then get at it."

He began stacking dishes; and when the last plates were on a tray, Tippy lingered behind to blow out the candles in the lamps.

Funny, she thought, I haven't remembered Ken so much today. It's all been Peter. I've even been jealous of Christy, and that's queer, too. Perhaps it's because Ken and I never did anything like this together. Oh, dear, I hope Alcie's surprise isn't a picnic. Ken and I were always going for tramps and taking a picnic lunch along.

She heard Peter coming back to find her, and leaned hastily over the lamps. "I'm almost finished," she said, as his arms went around her waist. "You blow one out."

He leaned over with her, his face close to hers, and it was all he could do to keep from pressing their cheeks together.

CHAPTER VIII

TIPPY sat on the front lawn under one of the big, old trees. She wore clean blue shorts and a starched white shirt with a red silk scarf knotted under the collar. Her back was bowed as she surveyed her arms and legs. "Puny," she said to Peter, who reclined comfortably in an old-fashioned hammock. "Pale and puny, that's me."

"Oh you weren't so bad, Tip," he answered. "They didn't beat us so much."

The morning had been taken up with tennis. Tippy and Peter had played on the smooth, fast court of the senior Draytons against Christy and her Roger Lynn. They had lost so many games that finally they had played against Christy and her little brother. After even that struggle had ended in ignominious defeat, Tippy had sat on the side lines and

95

watched while Peter played Roger, then Christy, and had laughingly but firmly refused to let any of them win a love set from her.

"I wasn't anything to brag about," she contended, still studying her right arm; and she said in wonderment, "I don't see what became of my muscles. You haven't played since you left here, but you sent the shots back."

"So did you—sometimes."

"With a weak plop that even little Keith could smack against the backstop. And I never seemed to be where I thought I was going. I never got there," she said with a rueful laugh. "I made swan dives and jackknives, and you must say I stirred up a breeze, just fanning the air. Zing would go the ball, and zing I'd go after it— and bump into you."

"More exercise is what you need," he answered, swinging his legs out of the hammock and sitting up. "Road work."

"What kind of road work? Digging ditches?"

"Walking. Alcie's tied up with party doings and hasn't time to fool with us. She has Mrs. Drayton's cook in there, so why don't we just pack ourselves a lunch and go on a picnic? She'd like nothing better than to be rid of us."

A picnic for two. Here it came, the thing she dreaded most. Tippy swallowed and took a deep breath before she said, "I don't think I—feel like taking any more exercise." And she pleaded silently, "Please, Peter, don't want me to do something Ken and I loved to do together. Don't make me go on a picnic with anyone but Ken."

But Peter sat on the edge of the hammock, his bare brown arms pressed down against it, his sneakers tapping the grass.

96

He saw the creamy texture of her skin that she so deplored fade even whiter along her cheeks and around her mouth, as he said, "A picnic's what the doctor ordered. You make up some sandwiches and I'll fix a thermos of coffee. We'll drive back into the woods and then start walking. Maybe we'll eat on a cliff above the Delaware. You can see miles from there."

Tippy sat with her lips pressed together. Her throat was tight and her heart lost somewhere within her. Callous Peter. He knew of her picnics with Ken. During those wretched days after the telegram had come, she had told him of the walks she and Ken had taken in Germany and of their last wonderful afternoon in Washington, when they had eaten their lunch on a high hill near the Potomac. Once Peter would have understood and not forced her to do something impossible.

"I'm sorry, Peter," she began, but he jumped up and pulled her to her feet.

"No muscles," he said lightly, gripping her arms under their short white sleeves. "Beautiful legs, but weak. Well, Uncle Peter's going to put you in the pink."

He propelled her toward the house; and although she protested silently, she made no audible comment. He can't hurt my memories, she thought. Perhaps I can dream up an errand in the village and we'll fool around so long that we'll have to eat in the car. Or maybe Alcie will have something she wants us to do.

But Alice was glad to have them go. "Hooray," she said frankly. "Jon always eats in town, so Bertha and I can whip

97

along faster with no dishes to wash. There's cold boiled ham you can have, and deviled eggs."

Peter whistled while he measured coffee into a percolator, but Tippy silently spread bread with mustard. Even Alice had let her down; and a loving little pat on her back only meant that Alice understood her plight but would do nothing to change it. Peter was her own dear brother, and Peter wanted a picnic. Besides, it relieved her of two troublesome guests. Tippy was still resentful as she followed Peter to the door, and she turned back to look stonily into two compassionate gray eyes.

She would go on the picnic. She would do what they both expected of her, but she would close her ears and her eyes and her heart. She would pretend she and Peter were eating in the Drayton yard.

There was no chance to stop in the village, for Peter met her suggestion with a noncommittal nod. "Later," he said, turning off on a side road in the opposite direction. "I think this takes us to the river. Seems to me I remember a fork where we can leave the car and climb a hill on foot. Feel strong enough?"

"I'm very strong."

She knew he was laughing at her; at the poor showing she had made against the flashing Christy whose brown legs carried her about the court like a comet, whose smile was so white it dazzled. There really was no comparison between the sun-baked Christy and the little working girl from town. "I don't see why you didn't take Christy on the picnic," she said petulantly, and made Peter laugh aloud.

"Chris doesn't need it," he replied, watching ruts in the narrow graveled road.

"And I suppose I do?"

"More than anyone I know." His hand left the wheel and rested on her clasped ones for a moment. "I'm looking after you, childie," he said.

"It's a funny looking-after." Her hands withdrew from under his and she rested one on the door as the car bounced. "I don't need scenery," she said suddenly, sitting up. "I *live* in the country."

"But you don't see it. Well, here we are." He pulled into a little glade and set his brake. "Now we do some climbing."

Tippy got out of the car almost stiff-legged and watched him take out the basket of lunch. "Peter," she said, making one last try and not caring how much he could read in her words, "Let's go back home. Please?"

"Up we go. If stones begin to slip, hang onto my belt. It's quite a climb as I remember it. I wish we had my tank, Kitten, here so you could see what she can do. I'll bet George Washington never would have waited to throw his dollar across the Delaware if he'd seen Kitten sitting on the cliff with her guns pointed at him. Wouldn't that have been something?"

He kept up a chatter of conversation, almost as fast as the rattle of stones that slid by them. Tippy concentrated on gaining ground without the aid of his belt, and the exertion left her no time for thoughts or even resentment. She was too busy scrambling for a foothold.

"Phew," she panted, when they reached the top, flopping down on rough grass, her arms limp at her sides. "I feel—like a—mountain goat."

"Some view, huh?" Peter dropped down, too, and wiped his forehead on his arm.

"I can't look." She rolled over on her face, not because she cared about a view now, but simply because she wanted her breath back and was ashamed to let him see her fighting for it.

"Softy," he teased, and bent over and kissed the childish curls on the back of her neck. "Here, have a swig of water. I brought a thermos of that, too. *Sit up!*"

"*Shut up.*" Tippy laughed in spite of herself. He had kissed the back of her neck. He was kind. She turned her face on her arm and peeked at him. "Here I am, half-dead," she said, "and you tell me to sit up and look around. Honestly!"

"Lie where you fell then," he retorted. "It's after one o'clock and hunger has set in on me. You'll pardon me if I eat, won't you?"

"No." She felt perverse. She was angry with him, still very angry, but he looked so dear sitting there, his yellow hair in hot little spikes and his T shirt pulled out in the back. He looked very strong and masculine. She slid a hand out from beneath her cheek, then pulled it back again. He looked interested in the lunch, too. "Don't pay any mind to me," she said, closing her eyes. "I'll just lie here and quietly die of heat prostra. . . . " A sandwich was stuffed between her teeth, so that she broke off, sputtering.

"Eat!" he commanded, watching her sit up and pick bread from her shirt. And he went on in the sweet tone used for children, "If you'll eat like a good little girl, Uncle Peter will tell you a story. Once upon a time. . . ."

"Once upon a time there was a mean old man, and I hate him," Tippy exploded. "He made a girl climb way up on a hill and was horrid to her. He made her so mad that she forgot she had ever liked him. She wanted to—she wanted to hit him."

"But she didn't," Peter filled in. "She couldn't. She was *pu-u-uny!*"

"She wasn't! She was just as strong as—as Christy Drayton," Tippy shouted back. "She only pretended to be that way because the great, big, strong, stupid man called her something silly, like 'childie!' *Childie!*"

"It's a very nice name—*I* think."

"It isn't. It's horrid." Tippy stared straight ahead of her and didn't even see the view. The broad river with its cliff and hills behind it might have been Fifth Avenue in New York, for all she noticed. The dreaded picnic had become a matter of snatching at chunks of bread and flinging them as far as she could. Her picnic partner was simply a childhood adversary. They were having their first quarrel, or rather, she was having it, for Peter simply sat and ate.

Now and then he put in word or two, simply to keep her going, for he thought she was having a beautiful tantrum. She needed one. And when her spluttering calmed down to such a pace that she sat with her knees hunched up and her chin resting on them, he said, "Blow another gasket, kid, it'll do you good."

Tippy slammed her legs out, straight. "I'm so *mad*," she cried, "I'm just so mad at *everything!*"

"I know how you feel," he answered, taking another bite of cake. "I get like that at Annabelle sometimes. I want to kick her wheels right out from under her."

"Hm." Tippy looked speculatively at his legs in old white cadet slacks, and he moved one closer to her.

"Kick it," he invited. And when she reached over and pinched until he let out a yell, he grabbed her hand and asked, "Feel better now?"

"I guess so. Oh, my goodness." She pulled up his trouser leg to see what damage she had done to his shin, and, finding none, shoved it down again. "Why, I haven't blown up like that in years," she said. "Things went round and round and I wanted to stamp my feet. They tell me that I was an awful foot-stamper when I was little. I used to lie on the floor and kick."

Peter silently held out another sandwich and she took it, even bit a piece from it without realizing she had put it in her mouth. "I haven't done it for years," she repeated, still surprised at her own behavior. "Not since I was old enough to know better and be ashamed of losing my temper. Why do you suppose I did it now—with you?"

"Childie," he used the word into an acceptant smile that curved her lips sweetly upward, as he said, "sometimes people take about all they can. Then they let some lightning loose, and don't know why or where it's going to hit."

"But to do it with you! Why would I be mad or cross with you?" she argued. "I never have been."

Peter wanted to say, "Because you never cared enough and because I never made you do something I knew would hurt you," but he only answered thoughtfully, "It's hard to tell. I teased you."

"You've always teased me. In a tender way, of course, not like Bobby did, and it never made me mad before. It rather pleased me. I liked having you think I was a—'softy,' till to-day."

"What made you change?"

"I don't know." Tippy looked down at her sandwich while she wondered what had made her want to seem more import-ant to Peter. The idea had first come to her as she sat beside the tennis court, watching Christy slam back the tennis balls. Peter's shout of, "Good shot, Chris, nice play," had made her wish she had kept up her own game, that she were out there showing off. She had felt unhappy and forlorn. "I don't know," she repeated, "but this is the queerest picnic I ever went on."

Peter refrained from saying it had been almost made to order. To manage one that would break the spell of Ken had seemed an impossible task, but something had helped him along. At least Tippy knew she was out with Peter Jordon and not leaning on a wailing wall, and he felt that he had accomplished a great deal. "I think we ought to go," he said, not tempting fate too far.

"But I haven't eaten."

"Are you hungry?"

"Well, of course I am. I'm starved." Tippy was already plowing through the basket he had partially repacked. "Why, you rat!" she cried. "You didn't save me an egg!"

"Down at the bottom. There's a piece of cake, too." He lit a cigarette and watched her spread her find around her. She munched and brushed crumbs off her face while she scuffled her feet back and forth in the coarse grass.

He left her to her thoughts, and was listening contentedly to the repeated call of a quail, when she turned her head and said, "You know something? I don't believe I'll ever be afraid of picnics again."

"That's good, Tip."

"Or of anything else I may have to do in life. Of course you didn't know it," she went on, "but I felt as if I simply couldn't come today. And then you made me. Now, I'm glad I did."

Peter wanted to tell her how well he had known it, but now was not the time. She had taken her first faint flutter on new wings and he must let her think she had done it alone. Perhaps the time would never come when he could say, "My darling, oh, how well I understood." So he lay back with his arms crossed under his head, and answered, "I'm glad you did, too, Tippy. I've wanted a time alone with you, like this. Hear that quail?"

"Where?" She lifted her head to listen.

The call was close, somewhere in the thick growth near them, and she said, "Funny. I didn't hear it. There are lots of sounds around us when we listen. Perhaps it's a mother quail calling her children away from such a dangerous spot."

"Hm-um, they just lead them away. Softly and carefully so we won't hear them." And he thought ruefully to himself, Old mother quail, that's me. I've led her this far, but, heck, where do we go from here?

Back home, it seemed, where his chances would dwindle again, for she was closing the basket. "We should help Alcie and Jon," she said. "We promised to set up the tables under the trees, and I have a dress to press." And then she added, "Peter, it's been a *good* picnic."

"Feel better?"

"I feel—remade." The words that followed seemed strange to even her own ears, for she said without understanding why, "I feel as if I want a chance at something. I don't know what it is, exactly, but I feel as if I have to pitch in and fight for it. Now what do you suppose I want to fight for?"

"Maybe it's Miss Turnbull's job."

"That?" she scoffed. "I wouldn't have it as a gift. It's something bigger."

She turned and studied his upturned face carefully. Sunlight slanted on it through the trees, marking the high cheekbones, the long line of jaw. A leaf made flickering shade for half-closed eyes, and she wanted to bend down and peek under the lowered lids. It was a new face, closed and still. One she had never truly seen before. And she said softly, "I'm going to put up a fight."

" 'Atta girl."

He sat up and brushed grass from his back, unconscious of the scrutiny he had just received, or its meaning. "Time to go," he said. "Are you ready?"

"All set but fastening the basket." Another fleeting memory touched her: another hill, another man, a different view and a knitting bag for the lunch instead of a basket. Then Peter ducked his head and smiled at her, and she took his hand for the downhill slide.

CHAPTER IX

"Oh, Tip," Alice cried, as Tippy danced down the stairway in a lace dress that billowed out like pale pink foam, "you remind me of strawberry mousse!"

"That's a compliment straight from the stomach," Tippy laughed as she returned graciously, "gastronomically speaking, you look like a stick of peppermint candy."

Alice's striped taffeta was just as full above her pretty legs as Tippy's. Her brown hair shone and she looked more like the hostess's carefree daughter than the hostess herself, and no one would have guessed that she had put in a full day at work. "We're all ready," she said. "Bertha's still frying the last of the chicken and Jon's cutting out some cartoons to use instead of place cards. He has the basement full of old magazines, and I found one for you that—oh, my soul, here they come!"

She darted to the door and back again to ask, "Since it's turned pretty cool, shall we have them come in here first and then go out? I do so love to show off the house. I feel so proud of it," she said, smiling possessively at the living room. "But it doesn't really matter. They can come in later, because I've planned to play a game if things bog down. You know, things do bog down sometimes at parties."

"Stop babbling." Tippy went down the last step and put her arm around Alice's waist. "You're nervous, friend," she teased. "Remember all the parties you gave on the Island? Nothing ever 'bogged down' there."

"But this is d-different," Alice stuttered. "This is our first sort of formal affair. Oh, Tippy," she clasped her hands together as a foursome started along the flagstone walk, and said earnestly, "I want it right for Jonathan. He's as excited as I am, and it has to be right. Who's coming? Can you see?"

"Four people Jon's known all his life and you've known ever since you met him. A girl named Kitty who was at your wedding and drops in almost every day, that homely, stringy guy you call Tink, and redheaded Sue Bell Van Sycle with a man I never saw before."

"He's—he's Roger Lynn's brother, Gregory." Alice answered, revived because three good friends were the first to arrive, and could take care of Gregory who was older and more serious. "Come on."

She let the screen door bang as she ran across the narrow, old-fashioned porch and down the steps. "Welcome," she cried, hugging the girls and Tink, and holding out a friendly hand to Gregory Lynn. "Tippy, you know everyone but Greg. He graduated from K State, and is a veterinarian, with an office and everything. Tink, go hunt up Jon and Peter. Oh, happy day in the morning, here come some more!"

Guests began to arrive faster than she could greet them. Jonathan directed them to a parking lot in the back yard and introduced Peter to his friends. Alice tried to count twenty-two heads moving about on the lawn, and when she was sure there were twenty-two with no duplicate addition, and the evening dusk was just right for lamps to be lighted on the tables and for farm lanterns Jonathan had hung in the branches of the trees to twinkle like stars, she dashed off to her kitchen.

Jonathan helped her arrange silver platters on a long table covered with their best lace cloth, a bowl of flowers in the center; and he almost shouted, "Come and get it," in their usual style, before he remembered that this was a party.

"How do you start 'em coming?" he asked; and she answered, busy with a tureen of fresh peas:

"You mingle. You walk around among them and delicately suggest that they fill their plates and hunt their cartoons. And," she looked up to say, "by the time you have them all settled, you rush back and load up the platters again."

"Don't *we* eat?" he asked. "It doesn't sound like much fun for us, does it?"

"Oh, we slide out and slide back, and since we're at separate tables, no one is ever conscious of our absences. Tippy and Chris said they'd help us change plates and carry out dessert, and we can count on Peter, so we aren't going to

109

starve. And when you do have to get up," she cautioned, knowing it was all new to him, this entertaining without servants, "don't be polite and say, 'Excuse me.' Just vanish."

"It looks like a good party—the kind Moth and Dad give. Oh, Alcie," he told her fervently, forgetting his guests, "you're wonderful. Gosh, I wish we could give parties like this once a month."

"I don't. Even with your mother buying the chickens for us, it cost like the dickens; my health wouldn't take it. I'm tired in the back."

"I'll do the dishes."

"Bertha will, and I gave Keith a dollar to help her. He said he'd empty the garbage and mop up the floor for a quarter extra, so we won't have to worry. Now, remember—circulate."

"There's food, folks," he practiced as they walked back. "Dinner is served." "Hey, you two, break it up and go fill your plates." And he asked anxiously, "Is that the way you meant?"

"Anything will do."

There was great merriment going on when they reached the group of trees, for someone had discovered the cartoons on the tables. Heads were bent over the lamps, and the whole carefully planned scheme seemed to be a jumble, for the little pictures were being passed around without any thought of their order. Tinker recognized himself with a guitar, but couldn't find at which table he belonged; a golfer refused to admit he struck such ridiculous poses and said he wanted to eat with the girl who ogled idiotically at a man behind a TV camera. Christy had a picture of a college girl waving a pennant. Tippy, giving it an amused glance, saw "Couple I, Table IV" written on the top of it. The numbers matched the ones on Peter's picture of a soldier eating a can of beans in a ditch, and she turned quickly away.

Jonathan tried to straighten things out. He and Alice shoved their guests into their rightful spots, and whatever remarks he made about the waiting dinner must have been entirely understandable and to the point, for off they swooped.

"I guess you and I are paired together," Roger Lynn said, walking across the lawn beside Tippy, and giving her a plate from a stack at the end of the table. "I'm glad."

"As long as it isn't tennis, I'm glad, too. I really suffered this morning," she said with a rueful smile, looking into his dark, pointed face.

"I wasn't so hot either," he answered, drumming on the bottom of his plate while they waited for the long line to move. "Christy pulled me through. She plays a lot." His gaze swept along ahead of him, and Tippy followed it to a tall light head and a shorter light one beside it. "My father's a playwright, as I suppose you know," he went on conversationally, "but he fancies himself a gentleman farmer. I'm the guy who has to run the farm so I keep pretty fit. I live over there with my brother Greg who's a vet."

"Do you like it?"

"Oh, so-so. I go into the navy next week."

There was a space before them, and they moved as far as

the mashed potatoes. Roger was pleasant, and Tippy liked him. He was quiet, too; and several times during dinner when he said, "I beg your pardon, I didn't hear you," she wondered if it were because he was listening to Christy's laughing banter at the next table, just as she was.

That foursome was very gay. On each side of Christy and Peter were the snub-nosed, redheaded Sue Bell and the homely, comical Tink. Tippy thought she had never heard Peter throw back his head and laugh so much. Her own table had a much too-loving bride and groom who had traded seats with other couples in order to be together, and but for the wink Roger sent her now and then and leaning over to snatch bits of merriment from those beside them, the dinner would have been too dull to bear.

But at last Alice arose like a true and gracious hostess. She walked among the tables, saying, "I thought we might play 'the game' for a little while, just while the tables are being cleared, if you'd like to, that is." She always added, "You don't have to if you'd rather not," but her grin was happy as they all trouped back to the house. It was really going well, and she and Jonathan gave each other a satisfied poke as they got out paper and pencils.

"Now this is the way we do it," Jonathan yelled. "Keep still a minute. Alcie's going to explain it because she hid the stuff. Alcie, where are you?"

"Here. On the footstool, so I can see. Look, everyone. There's a list of objects written on these pieces of paper. Nine objects, I think. Yep, nine. Every one is in plain sight, remember that, Plain sight! All you have to do is write down on your paper where you saw it. Don't touch it. And my advice to you is, don't let anyone else know when you find something. Just walk off to write it down. Is that clear?"

"Sure," someone called, "like mud. Is all the stuff inside the house?"

"It's either in this room or the library," she answered, pointing. "Just these two rooms. Not in the hall, or dining room, or anywhere else. And you're to go in couples. I thought," she said with a grin, conscious of the two she had mismated at dinner, "since it's leap year, I'd let the girls choose their partners. Are there any questions?"

No one could think of anything to ask, not until each had read his list and found a partner, so she passed a slip of paper and a pencil down to the girls around her and waited for the barrage to start.

Tippy took her set and turned to look for Peter. She was among the last to receive it from Alice, although she had reached up for it with the rest. She pushed back through the crowd and saw him, far over by the piano, already studying his printed instructions with Christy. Roger was spoken for, and Tink, the only ones she knew really well, so she was left standing on the edge of things, uncomfortable and not liking Jonathan's sister quite as well as she always had.

"I guess you'll have to take me," a voice beside her said, and she turned to look at Gregory.

It seemed to be a night of Lynns. Gregory was pleasant and blond, and wore glasses. His eyes had an intelligent look behind their bone-rimmed frames and she gave him a smile of genuine pleasure. If she couldn't be with Peter, it might be fun to have a partner who would help her win. "Fine," she said. "Let's read what we're to look for."

They bent their heads as the others were doing and joined in the chorus of questions. Where could such peculiar things be hidden? Tippy ran her finger down the list as she read it aloud. "Bobby pin. Hairpin. Penny. Wedding ring. Dollar bill. Thimble. Postage stamp. Paper clip. Safety pin." Such small objects to elude the eye.

Other couples had begun to hunt. The living room swarmed with avid seekers, and Alice and Jonathan had taken their posts by the library door where they could watch both rooms.

"We'd better do the library while it's empty," Tippy suggested, not finding Peter anywhere in the crowd that milled around her. "Do you—think that's a good idea?"

"Suits me." Gregory wandered toward the door, watching peoples' faces for clues as he went, when Tippy wanted to run.

She was relieved to find Peter decorously bent over a small table on one side of the room while Christy inspected a lamp with a fluted shade on the other. It was such a pleasant sight that she said gayly, "Any luck?"

"Not a thing." Peter gave her a blank stare and turned so quickly from the spot where he had been that she hurried over. There must be something there, she thought, studying a book, a bonbon dish, and a plant in a large blue pot.

She stared fixedly at each in turn, looking for something that didn't belong there, while the room filled up behind her. Then she, too, turned and sauntered off.

"Greg," she whispered, pulling her puzzled partner up

114

from a search along the baseboard beside the mantel, "there's a dollar bill all squashed up and tucked in the leaves of that bushy green plant. Shall I write it down or wait?"

"Better wait," he cautioned. "Do you see anything on this fire set?"

Tippy squatted down beside him and forgot Peter in the fun of hunting for some strange object. The fire set was as shiny as brass should be and as unadorned. They moved reluctantly on, and their list refused to grow again.

"Alcie," she asked, as they left the library for a larger hunting ground, "are you sure you hid all the things you think you did?"

"Sure as sure," Alice laughed. "I've been looking at peoples' papers, and every single item has been found. Not all by the same couples," she said. "Some have one thing, some another, but they've all been found."

"Well, I can't see them."

Gregory had seated himself on the arm of a chair and was watching the other contestants work. When someone inspected a floor lamp and turned quickly away, he hopped up and went over. "Write down thimble," he said, coming back to Tippy, who was down before another fireplace. "The lamp over there has something that looks like a gold switch on its base. Darned if I'd have seen it, if I hadn't been watching Jim Severson. I'll go back to my post."

He studied faces while Tippy searched. Together, they managed to find a number of items, and were doing very well when Alice mounted her footstool again and called, "Kitty and Tink have them all. Stop hunting, the game's all over."

"It's all over!" Jonathan echoed her from the library, and people came running with groans of disappointment.

"Just give us another minute," Christy pleaded. "Peter and I have everything but one."

"Too late." Alice shook her head and held up two tissue-wrapped packages that held current, best-selling novels. "Here, Kitty, Tink," she said. "You won. Step up and claim your prizes."

"Well, at least tell us where they found the stuff," someone shouted. "I don't believe it."

"All right," she laughed. "We'll even show you."

She hopped down from her stool and went over to the Venetian blind. "Here's the postage stamp," she said, "pasted around the little knob on the end of the cord. Can you see it?"

"Now I do," Tippy groaned to Gregory.

But Peter answered smugly from her other side. "We found it. Carry on, Alcie."

"And the hairpin's hanging in the wire mesh of this fire-screen," Alice demonstrated, lifting it out and holding it up. "And the wedding ring may look like a band around this lamp where the shade fits on, but if you unscrew the fancy knob, you have the ring. It isn't mine, by the way. I bought it in a ten cent store, so anyone may have it." She tossed the ring into the center of a group, and Peter picked it out of the air.

"Too small for me," he said, and passed it on to Tippy. "Show us some more, Alcie."

"The dollar bill's in the philodendron plant, the safety pin seems to be holding one of my fine new slip covers together, but I assure you it isn't," she went on. "The penny's on the gold face of that electric clock over there, and covering the round hole that's usually red. Jon took off the glass and put it back, and I hope he can fix it again. The paper clip's just stuck in the fluting of a lamp in the library, and the bobby pin's lying along the frame of that painting over the mantel."

Gregory went to look at the painting. "Darned if it isn't," he said, pushing it off. "It looked just like a line under the artist's signature. Smart hiding."

People had begun to move around, to see the puzzling items for themselves, but Peter stood looking at Tippy. "How did you do?" he asked.

"Not very well. I thought Gregory would be good, when I chose him," she answered, a little ashamed of her false statement but trying to keep her pride from crumbling. "But he wasn't. What he found, he found from watching others."

"I wasn't any help to Chris, either." Peter didn't say he had been watching others, too, one other, and he left Tippy tearing up her list while he turned to answer a girl who called to him.

The game was ended but Alice had another idea. She seemed full of ideas tonight, Tippy thought dolefully, watching her hand Tinker a guitar and prepare to herd her docile sheep outside again.

They went in a drove. A few wandered idly, as sheep will do, but the majority followed her back to the overhanging grove of trees, and the rugs and chairs and pillows. Tippy went along beside Gregory who seemed to feel they had somehow become attached. He really belonged with the young married crowd, and she wondered why he stayed with her. She even sat down on the fringe of things and quietly asked him.

Not for worlds would she have joined Peter and Christy, who were in the group surrounding Tink and the soft, plinking sounds he made. Now and then he let his instrument lie across his knees, and it was hard to tell when his own voice filled in the notes. "Sing," he commanded, and the quiet night was filled with voices. Tippy and Greg sat talking on.

"Aren't you coming over?" Peter looked down at her to ask when she least expected him to. She hadn't seen him leave his group, and there he was above her.

"After a while," she answered, almost snubbing him in her surprise. "Greg's telling me why he wanted to be a veterinarian. He likes animals so much."

"Make it soon," he said with a pat on her shoulder, and went back to the music.

He didn't go back to Christy, though, she noticed, for Christy had walked away and was headed for the house.

It was quite dark on the deserted lawn, and although Tippy couldn't see her, Christy hurried. "Hey," she called to Alice, who had just switched out the kitchen lights and was standing on the back step, "I turn in my suit. I quit, I resign."

"But you can't," Alice gasped. "Things are going *wonderfully!* Tippy doesn't do anything but watch Peter. She couldn't even hunt for hunting him. Oh, you *can't* quit, *now!*"

"I can't? Sister dear, I have." Christy sat down on the

stone step and said earnestly, "Look, honey, Roger goes in the navy next week and I go back to college. I've wasted a whole morning and evening on Peter. He's a darling," she said hastily, "and I could enjoy him no end, week after next. You know he doesn't care a whoop for anyone but Tippy, and it's been Roger for me ever since we moved here. Call it propinquity or anything you like, but there we both are. And Roger's beginning to champ at the bit. We haven't had much fun tonight."

"But it's working so well." Alice sighed and sat down, too. "Tippy's just *miserable*, I know she is."

"Cheerful thought." Christy laughed but remained determined. "I'm going to hunt up my own young man," she said, "and take what's left of the evening. He understands about the good deed I'm supposed to be doing, but he isn't happy about it. And I don't want Tippy to hate me. I don't," she said earnestly. "I'm not that kind of girl, Alcie, and you know it."

"I suppose not." Alice released a sigh. "What about tomorrow?" she asked.

"Include me out. Roger and I have plans of our own for tomorrow."

"All right." Alice stood up and said, looking off into the trees, "They're going home now, anyway. Thanks for all you've done. You've been a wonderful help, Chris."

"I hope I can explain it to Tippy someday."

Christy got up, too, and they walked slowly out to meet the good nights. "I won't be seeing you again, Tippy," she said, knowing how inadequate the words were. "I'm going to a ball game in Philly tomorrow, but shall I give you a ring sometime when I come in town?"

"We could lunch together." Tippy smiled an honest little smile that Christy hoped was a forgiving one. She also hoped it wouldn't be too long before she knew.

"See you then," she said, and turned away to look for Roger.

Tippy was left shaking hands as one of the guests of honor. She walked back to the house with a girl to find the summer wrap she had left inside, and when the last car had gone, stayed for a moment alone on the porch.

She could see Alice emptying ash trays in the living room, gathering up her pencils and tossing the pieces of wasted paper into the fireplace. It was dark and still outside, with only the sound of motors fading in the distance. A firefly winked his lantern at her, and she leaned against one of the thin old pillars of the porch. Her hands were clasped behind her and she stared out into the black, thickly studded sky, wanting Peter to come around the house, willing him to come.

And then she heard his voice inside. He and Jonathan had come in the back door together. She whirled around to see him leaning against the mantel, talking of the party. His gray jacket was unbuttoned and his thumbs were hooked in his belt, the fingers spread along his hips in a flat, familiar gesture. In a dear gesture, she thought miserably, wishing he could see how lonely she looked, standing off alone. But he was grinning at Alice who shook her pencils at him; and she could hear him say, "What were you trying to do, chum?" and Alice was laughing.

"She's no cupid," Jonathan answered for her, going to dump ashes into a bowl and rumpling her hair as he passed her. "But she's cute as a hostess. Some party, hm?"

"Swell. Where's Tip?" Peter had finally remembered her. "Did she come in?" he asked.

"Search me. Maybe she's gone to bed."

Jonathan went on about his duties, talking the evening over with Alice, while Peter stood looking at the ceiling and listening for any sounds upstairs.

"I don't think she came in," he said. "Maybe I'd better take a look around."

He started for the door, and Tippy dashed across the porch to sit on the step. "Oh, hello," she said, looking over her shoulder. "It's lovely out. Perhaps I should help Alcie, though."

"She's almost through." He walked out and stood above her. "It is a nice night," he said. "Romantic. Which reminds me. What did you do with the handsome ring I gave you?"

"It's on a table somewhere." Not for worlds would she have added that it was safely tucked in the little evening bag she had carried. "Why? Do you want it back?"

"Of course not. It's a present."

"I thank you. Shall I wear it on a chain around my neck? Like a beautiful secret?" she asked, looking up.

The hall light streamed out and showed her mouth smiling and her eyes full of laughter. She felt bubbling over because Peter was near her again, but he couldn't know that.

"Never be without it," he answered lightly, ignoring the place she patted on the step beside her. "Witches' curses will haunt you if you do. How about a glass of milk and a piece of cake before we go to bed?"

"All right." She jumped up as if she were in a greater hurry than he was, and very hungry. But she felt so disappointed and rebuffed that she silently vowed to throw away the darned old ring tomorrow.

CHAPTER X

"Good morning, darlings," Tippy caroled, coming into the kitchen where Alice and Jonathan sat at breakfast. "Wonderful party last night, wonderful country air for sleeping, and one of the most beautiful mornings I ever saw."

"Hi." Jonathan laid down his newspaper and got up to move a chrome and yellow leather stool over to the table for her, and Alice dropped a piece of bread into the toaster and pressed down the lever.

"The cereal's on the sink, pet." she said. "Choose your kind."

"Thanks." Tippy poured flakes from a box into a yellow bowl and carried it back to the table. "Where's your big brother?" she asked casually, reaching for the sugar bowl.

"Being lazy, I suppose. I think I heard him banging around up there." Alice cocked her head and listened. "What could he be doing?" she wondered.

At her words, the old stairway creaked as if each individual step was having its back broken, and the dining room floor groaned. The swinging door flew open and Peter came to a smart salute. "Lieutenant Jordon reporting," he said.

"At ease." Jonathan brought the kitchen stool, which was the only seat left, and set it beside Tippy. "You want to sit by your girl friend?" he asked. "Or shall I swap places with you?"

"I want to sit with Tippy. *Right* beside her." Peter perched on the stool and looked down on the smooth curls below him. "Good morning, beautiful," he said.

"The same to you, Prince Charming. Have some orange juice and collect yourself." She held up a glass and he leaned over and took a sip from it. "Oh, not that way, you big baby," she scolded. "Put out your little hands and take it."

"They're cold," he complained. "They might drop it."

She set the glass before him and considered his white T shirt. "If you'd put on more clothes," she said virtuously, "you wouldn't mind a sudden change in temperature. *I* have on a sweater."

"And *I* have on long pants. Your poor blue legs have prickles on 'em," he retorted, leaning toward the plate of bacon and eggs Alice had ready for him. "Thanks, sister, dear. Now that you've banged around down here and wakened us all, what do we do with our day?" he asked.

"We have our big surprise. Oh, golly, Jon, you tell them." Alice stopped buttering a piece of toast and looked at Jonathan who was carefully separating the comic section of his paper into four equal parts. "The horses belong to your family."

"*Horses?*" Tippy's and Peter's voices came out together. Tippy's was a horrified squeak and Peter's a lower rendition of shock.

"What, in Sam hill, do we do with horses?" he asked.

"We always ride on Sunday," Jonathan answered, grinning because he hadn't thought the novel plan would go over. "The folks have a batch of horses, and Alcie and I always ride."

"They used to belong to Cousin Edgar," Alice said, too eager to wait. "That's Mr. Coddington, the man who left Jon's family the house. He got to be a nut on horses, and when he died he left a lot of money for their support. They can't be sold or anything. They're just supposed to be ridden and taken care of as long as they live. One belongs to Christy, and there are two that Jon and I ride, and then there's Blossom who doesn't belong to anybody, really, and Beau Geste who just plays around in a pasture because he was Mr. Coddington's special favorite. Christy's going to lend us hers, and. . . ."

"Nobody's going to lend me one," Peter answered, watching Tippy shrink to half her size beside him.

"But you always loved horses so!" Alice cried. "You rode Royal, and you curried him and were so fussy about him."

"I made him a sacred promise," Peter said solemnly, laying down his fork and folding his hands on the table. "When we had to give him away, I promised him, 'Royal, old pal, never will my legs bestride a horse again. Never will I cluck and chirp or spur one on to a flying pace.' You wouldn't have me break my vow to Royal, would you?"

"Yes, I would—because I don't believe it anyway." Alice looked at Tippy and said, *"You* want to ride today, don't you, honey?"

"I do not," Tippy answered promptly. "I've never met any horse but Royal and I rode behind him in your carriage. The only horse I ever rode on top of was a pony. I was three years old and he belonged to Bobby. No, thank you."

"Aw, Tip." Alice saw Jonathan laughing and made a face at him. "Come on," she begged. "Try it today."

"And risk my life and limb? to say nothing of crawling around on all fours tomorrow, full of aches and pains? Your thoughtful planning for my nervous breakup overcomes me."

"You and Jon go on and ride," Peter backed her up by saying. "The old folks can stay home and play croquet."

"Jon." Alice looked pleadingly across the table but Jonathan surprised her, too.

"Let's go to the beach instead," he suggested. "We had that as our reserve, you know. Cold fried chicken from last night and some sandwiches mixed with sand after a swim would taste pretty good."

"And I'll blow you all to dinner in a hotel," Peter put in as a special inducement; while Tippy offered quickly:

"I'll make the beds and pack the lunch. I'll do all the work and turn cartwheels on the lawn if you just won't make me ride a horse."

"Well," Alice gave in graciously by conceding, "it might be more fun at that. Mike and Beany Wilson have a cottage over on Long Beach Island, and they're always begging us to come. They'll probably be out fishing but we can change to our bathing suits there and go off on our own."

"Yep, let's not mix up with strangers," Peter growled. "I have a date with Tippy today." And he looked down to reprimand, "You aren't eating your breakfast, little girl. Eat, or Papa'll say he wants to ride a horse."

"Then Papa will be stuck with a ride—all by himself." Tippy spread some jam on a piece of toast and flicked her lashes at him. "I don't think Papa would like that, do you?"

"You can bet your sweet life he wouldn't. How long does it take to get to this haven by the sea?"

"A couple of hours at the most, if traffic's heavy," Jonathan answered.

"Then let's get started."

Peter piled cups and saucers on a tray, said to Tippy, "If

you haven't finished by now you're out of luck," and took her plate. She dashed off to make the beds while Alice started packing a lunch and Jonathan went out to the garage to look for a thermos jug.

In less than an hour they were off; and before the sun remembered that this was still late August and he had quite a number of expectant bathers to burn, they were rattling over a chain of wooden causeways that spanned a bay, toward the distant booming of the sea.

The Wilsons, as Peter had hoped, were not at home; but two small dressing rooms and a shower in their garage were unlocked and fully equipped for itinerant bathers, so no one needed them. The dune before their cottage was like a round, bald head with a few tufts of green hair sprouting up, and the long white beach beyond was being gently washed by a blue sea edged with lacy ruffles.

"Last one down. . . ." Tippy shouted, and then remembered she still had a forfeit to collect. And while she hesitated over finishing the second challenge, the other three shot by her.

"You're the ring-tailed monkey," Alice hooted, dropping towels and a beach bag. "You'll have to go back to the car for my sunglasses when I want them."

"And you can put out the lunch," Jonathan added, handing her the basket.

Peter just stood and grinned. "Forfeit delayed," he said in such a low tone that Tippy felt a delightful quiver of anticipation.

He wasn't pining for Christy! At least he didn't seem to

128

be, for he flopped down beside her on a large striped beach towel and watched Alice and Jonathan run into the surf. "This is a perfect day," he said, squinting over the dazzling sea at a small fishing boat, far out against the sky. "Sometime I'd like to own a cottage at a place like this."

"I would, too. I'd like to have a sturdy little cottage, not behind a dune, but built right above the water and bulk-headed, like a lot of people have them. Like that one way down there," she pointed. "And I'd have heat in it so I could come down in winter and listen to the ocean boom and bang. We aren't so very far from the sea at home," she said. "Perhaps we could drive over to one of our beaches next Sunday."

"I'll have to be in Washington next week end, Tip," he answered.

"Why?"

"I have to go down tomorrow. I planned it as part of my trip, and I suppose it's really the important part. It's the reason I took this leave, and I guess you might say my future hinges on it."

"Oh." She sifted sand through her fingers as she asked, "How do you mean?"

"Well, it's kind of a story." He let his arms hang over his knees and stared fixedly at the mound of sand that covered his feet as he explained, "I was plenty mixed up before I came East. Dad's on that military mission in Turkey, you know, and he thinks it's an important spot just now, and interesting and pretty hot, from a military view. I'm due for overseas and he wants me to come over there. I can't quite see it because

—well, I've got my combat record to think of. Combat's necessary to an officer. I'm slated to go to FECOM—Far Eastern Command," he explained, since she had been so long out of the army, "but when a major general asks for a lieutenant, he usually gets him. Dad could ask, but he's waiting. He said he'd let me make up my own mind, and he wants me to talk things over with General Reed, who's a friend of his, and with a Colonel Clark. I said I would, this week, and make a decision."

"Would it take you all week?"

"I don't know." The sand hill cracked as he moved a foot and he bent over to remold it. "Gil McKettrick, my roommate at the Point, you know, is in the Pentagon and has a little apartment with a couple of other classmates, and they want me to bunk in for a few days. I told 'em I would."

"I see." Tippy slid back against the dune, away from him. Unmindful of the sand that slipped into her hair, she clasped her hands behind her head and asked the sky, "Do you think you'd rather go to Turkey, Peter?"

"In some ways, sure. I'd have a house, or an apartment, or something in Ankara. Not necessarily near Dad; but, between us, we might manage to bring the kids over. There are a lot of wives over there. That part appeals to me," he said slowly, "having a family life again. But I don't know. It might get awfully lonesome."

Tippy closed her eyes against the sun, and against his bare, bowed back. He went on packing sand, smoothing, patting, until his legs were covered, while she sat in silence, wondering helplessly what she should say to him. Finally he turned his head and looked at her over his shoulder.

"Have you gone to sleep?" he asked; and she could only shake her head.

He was going off to Washington. For a whole week. He was taking seven days from their short time together. And then he was going to FECOM, or to EUCOM. Just like that. "I'm due for overseas," he had said. "I'm leaving town, I'm leaving the country, I'm taking a short walk to the grocery store. Good-by, good luck, and God bless you." Well!

A ragged sigh escaped but was lost on the roll of a wave that washed in with a mighty splatter. She wondered what would happen if she slid back down to him and said persuasively, "Peter, don't stay so long in Washington." Would he say, "All right, Tippy, I'll hurry as fast as I can."? Or would he shake his head and say, "Sorry, but I want to."? She decided to try it.

But once beside him again it was hard to start. He grinned at her, said, "Hello, are you back again?" and put a peak on the castle where his legs had been.

"I was wondering," she began, "if Turkey, and going in for intelligence work wouldn't be a very good thing to have on your record."

"That's what your father thought."

"You've talked it over with Dad?"

"Oh, sure, the first night I was here. He gave me a lot of good slants."

"Which does he want you to do?"

"He said that's up to me." And, Peter thought, I hoped it

would be up to you, too. His castle was finished. "Pretty," he said, and moved his legs apart. Sand tumbled into a widening crack, much as his dreams had done, and he swung around to his knees. "Let's swim," he said, brushing off his bathing trunks and reaching for her cap. "Let's go way out beyond the surf where Alcie and Jon are and ride the waves."

Tippy took the white cap and held it. He was so close to her, there on his knees. She started to put it on, then dropped it onto the flaring blue ruffle that passed for a skirt on her bathing suit, and said in urgent desperation, "Peter, could I collect my forfeit now?"

"I guess you could." He looked at the two bobbing heads almost lost behind the spray of surf, and leaned forward on his hands. "It's private enough," he decided, his grin slow and amused. "I'm willing to pay up now."

But Tippy drew away. "*Willing?*" she cried. "Oh, Peter."

Her lips trembled and he wanted so much to kiss them. But what if this were only a mood with her, brought on by the sun and sand and sea, by the thought of his going away? By the kind attentiveness of Christy? He had no vanity, but he did have a heart that had been hurt too often. "Silly childie," he said, "to be so serious about a kiss. I want very much to kiss you. Does that satisfy you?"

"Not—now." She pulled the beach bag toward her and rummaged in it to hide two sudden tears that pushed through her lashes. "I'd rather swim," she said.

"After the kiss."

He took her face between his hands and pulled it up to

132

meet his. "Oh, childie," he said, seeing the shining drops, "I didn't mean to tease you. Forgive me, darling." And he gently kissed her eyelids.

Tippy's hands reached upward, then dropped again, for his lips had left her face. That's all the kiss there's going to be, she thought woefully. Just two little pecks on my eyes. I've used up my forfeit and I'm nowhere. I've lost him, somehow. Maybe to a girl in Texas—maybe because I couldn't make up my mind sooner.

"Go away," she said, and pushed against his chest. "I want to lie here in the sun and sleep."

She rolled over on her stomach, her face buried in her arms. Peter sat down to watch her. A little smile played around his mouth, was lost in a look of fear, then popped out to twitch his lips again. What if he were on the right track? he wondered. It seemed as if he might be. She had wanted to kiss him, and she never had really wanted to before. He reached across her for the beach bag and took out his cigarettes and lighter. Now what to do? Stick to a whole week in Washington or come back early and keep on trying? He looked at the back of her bright head and wished he could ask her. "Tippy," he wanted to say, "which is the best way for me to do? Accept the Turkey deal so we can be married, or go off and try to forget you? Shall I go to Washington and hope you'll be lonesome for me, or stick around and take my chances? I was pretty harsh and brutal yesterday, and did it do any good?"

Her face stayed hidden in her arms, so he sat blowing smoke while he worked at his knotty problem.

There wasn't really any way to figure it out, so he obeyed his longing and slid closer to her.

"I think I'll claim *my* forfeit now," he said, twisting her around. "Sit up, childie, and take your medicine." And he pressed their lips roughly together.

CHAPTER XI

"I'll drop you off at the studio, Tip, and take the car on to the parking lot," Peter said on Monday morning, as they came out of the Lincoln Tunnel. "I'd like to catch a train for Washington around noon."

"But what about your bag?"

"I'll leave it with you. If you don't mind taking care of it for me, I'll pick it up on my way to the station. I can tell you good-by that way."

"Oh, Peter, would you?" It sounded as if she were asking a favor, and Tippy hated herself for it.

The whole of yesterday had matched her other two with Peter, except that Christy was absent. He had been tender, sweet and thoughtful, nothing more, and there had been times when she was even jealous of Alice. Alice had had two men beaming admiringly upon her. When Alice needed a towel both Peter and Jonathan handed her one. Both put sun-tan lotion on her back and listened to her conversation as if she were stringing words of wisdom on golden chains to hang around their necks. It was all very fine for a young, new husband to do, Tippy morosely granted her that, but no brother, or even a sort of brother through a family marriage, should stick to her like a postage stamp. Four people out on a holiday were two too many.

"If I don't see you before you leave," she said, "you'll find your bag in Miss Turnbull's office."

"Right." He stopped for a traffic light and looked at the majestic buildings on each side of him. "What a place to live," he said. "Anyone can have it who wants it. Why are you so keen on it?"

"I'm not. I simply work here. There's my building over there and the light's changing."

He pulled the car out of the crawling traffic and eased it over to the curb. "If you'll sit here in case a cop comes by," he said, "I'll take my kit up."

"I can manage." Tippy stepped out and yanked the heavy canvas bag from the back seat. She knew the elevator starter would leave his post and take it from her, once she was inside the door, but it was medicine for her misery to have Peter see her stagger away with his luggage.

"By," she called. "Thanks for a lovely week end."

She didn't wait to see if the car pulled safely out or had its fenders bashed. She did hear Peter call, "I'll have to give you the parking ticket," but a revolving door was spinning her into her workaday world, and she had to be ready to spring out and not go around again. It would be just her luck, she thought, to have some man give the thing a push that would send her on the whole swift circuit again and make Peter think she'd come back on purpose.

She passed her bag over to her favorite starter, as she always did the boxes and bundles she brought in for the studio, and rode up beside it. It looked like the ghost of Peter, sitting there, pompous and important. And she pushed it out with her shoe when she reached her floor, then stumbled over it.

"Here," she said to Jimmy, a toothy boy who was always near the elevator doors at this hour, helpful and hoping for tips, "put this in my office."

"Miss Turnbull's back," he volunteered, as they bumped along together. "Sure you want it in there?"

"It will have to be."

Where else could Peter tell her good-by? Where else could she hang around and wait for him? Not at the reception desk. She sailed along the corridor and steeled herself for a day with her boss.

Miss Turnbull had her crutches and a lighter cast on her leg. She looked more like a poodle to Tippy than ever, after a whole week of not having seen her at all, and she wore more beads and bangles than usual. She had the office in a turmoil of sketches and small props; and after Tippy had done the best she could with a surprised welcome of return, she cut off any wasted pleasantries and plunged into work.

"Friday's set was bad," she snapped, "very bad. You forgot the sewing basket that's always on the little table, left. The ironing board was at least six inches out of line, and the Morris chair, right center, rumpled the rug."

It had been a very good set. Tippy had received congratulations on it and on the changes she had made from the sketches. Its success had sent her off for her week end with warm feeling for *A Lantern of Love* and the actors in it, who were only cross because they were as tired as she was. "I'll check it," she said acceptantly. "We're using it again today."

"Which I know. And Mr. Lovell wants to see you, so you'd better go to him right now. I'll have to manage alone."

No more tyrannical director ever lived than Mr. Lovell, or one who jumped about or screamed more. Tippy had often wished she could show him the calm, smooth way in which Josh worked; but as she left Miss Turnbull in the chaos she had created for herself in such a few minutes, she could only wonder what he wanted of her.

She found him in the big barn of Studio One, prancing up and down through a confusion of chairs and musical instruments a hillbilly band would use at eleven o'clock, mopping a handkerchief over what little gray hair he had, and jerking the thin, taut muscles along his narrow jaw.

"Ah, Miss Parrish," he said, hopping over an artificial stump and gripping both her hands. "At last you're here."

He had never greeted her so effusively before; in fact, he had never greeted her at all except with an order for something, and Tippy tried to free her hands that he pumped up and down. "Did you want something, Mr. Lovell?" she asked, wondering what he had suffered over the week end that could put him in such a state.

"Ah, yes. The actors will be here for rehearsal in—ah . . ."

he did release her to look at his wrist watch ". . . exactly fifteen minutes. The young lady who was to start the small new part of Minerva today has been taken to a hospital for an emergency operation. There is no time to find anyone else, so you must go on."

"Me? Oh, Mr. Lovell, not *me!*" Tippy began to back away and shake her head. "Why, I'd ruin you soap opera," she said. And at his wince of pain, she amended, "I mean your play, your episode. Why, I'd simply knock it into a cocked hat, that's all. I'd hash it all up, I mean. Oh, dear."

She was hurting him more and more with her slang, so she took a deep breath and started all over. "Mr. Lovell," she said, pressing her hand flat on her chest and looking straight between his narrow eyes, "I can't act. I couldn't walk on and off a stage, let alone speak."

"Ah, your family has the divine fire. You are very much like your sister," he protested.

"But I'm not my sister." For one horrified second Tippy thought he might have hoped she would drag in the famous Penny to save his show, his episode, then she saw he was too distraught to have clutched at that. And she felt more sympathetic toward him as she tried to explain, "I wouldn't be any good to you, Mr. Lovell. You'll have to find someone else. Think of someone, quick! The agencies have actors. That's what they're for."

"One came. She was awful. She plays in musicals. And now there isn't time for more telephoning and sending out calls. No," he said beating his brow with the agony of it all, "you will have to do. No matter how bad you are—and I

139

believe now that you will be very bad—you will have to save my play."

"No, I won't." Tippy wanted to hammer on her own head or tear out her hair, but she said as calmly as she could, "I'm not engaged by WRIP to act. I don't belong to the Actors Equity and I don't want to join it. Minerva goes through the serial for the next two weeks, and—and . . . I'm giving up my job. I'm leaving WRIP to—to be married."

The decision startled her as much as it did him. It was so sudden to both of them. They stared at each other as if their eyes were locked, and Tippy was the first to break away. "Oh, Mr. Lovell," she cried, as an inspiration struck her, "I have a girl for you! Now stand right there. Don't move." She wanted to hug him, and she did bounce him a little by his arms, before she sped away.

"Stephanie!" she shouted in the corridor leading to the library. "*Stephanie!*" She didn't care how much noise she made in this sanctimonious place. She was leaving, wasn't she? She had told Mr. Lovell she was—and she was. To be married? Hah. She didn't even have a bridegroom. But she was leaving. Oh, joy, joy, joy! Why hadn't she thought of it before? And Stephanie would have a part.

"Stephanie Miller, where are you?" she cried, flinging herself around the door. "Oh, there you are! Get down off that ladder this minute and go out and do your best for old Lovell. Act, girl, emote. You're in!"

"Tippy, are you crazy?"

Stephanie looked down from her ladder before the record folios, and Tippy gave the rungs a little shake. "Get down or

140

I'll knock you down," she said, laughing with excitement and happiness for the girl who had saved her date with Peter. "You're going on TV this afternoon. *Come down!*"

Stephanie descended shakily. Something good had happened, that was plain to see; for when she reached the floor, Tippy spun her about in a dance that hit the ladder and knocked a record from its top.

"Pay it no mind!" Tippy ordered as it broke, pushing her toward the door. "Lovell's waiting for you. You're to be Minerva for at least two weeks. And you'll keep coming in and coming in for years and years. By gum, you *look* like Minerva. I never saw her but you do."

By the time Tippy had led her across the studio and deposited her before the waiting director, Stephanie was almost as shattered as the record she had left on the floor.

"Here's your Minerva," Tippy cried, almost bumping them together as an introduction. "I told you I'd find her."

"But Minerva must be a blonde."

"She'll bleach her hair, won't you, Steph?"

"Why, yes, I guess so. If I've time, that is."

"Or she can wear a wig for today. How about it, Mr. Lovell? Isn't she pretty?"

Tippy was trying hard to make a sale. She felt like a dealer exhibiting the highlights on a jewel as she said, "She's so graceful and lovely, and she has such a beautiful voice." Silence from both of them answered her, and she urged with a little nudge, "Say something, Steph."

"Shall I read the part for you, Mr. Lovell?" There was

music in the way Stephanie said the words. She was suddenly ready to grasp her unexpected opportunity, and more than equal to it.

Tippy gave a satisfied sigh and Mr. Lovell looked less glum.

It was time for the successful casting agent to bow out and consider her own impulsive decision. So Tippy eased herself toward the door. "I'll leave you now," she mumbled, but Mr. Lovell's voice caught up with her.

"Good-by, Miss Parrish," he called. "Thank you for your assistance—and may your marriage be a happy one."

She fled. She was free. Not today, of course, perhaps not even tomorrow, for one never walked off a job without giving notice. But soon. She had found Stephanie for Mr. Lovell, so surely she could find a replacement for herself. There must be someone waiting around in an agency who had two hands and a pair of good strong legs, which were all Miss Turnbull needed. It didn't matter what kind of head was fastened on top of her running mechanism, so long as it sent out impulses that her arms and legs obeyed.

Tippy stopped in the hall to consider how she should break the news to her boss, and when. "Right now," she decided. A new feeling of independence was born within her. She might even escort Peter to his train. Eleven-thirty-to-almost-one would make a very good lunch hour, indeed. It would be a pleasant interlude in the middle of a busy day. So she walked slowly down the winding stairway and prepared her retirement speech.

The cluttered office looked just the same, except that a

wheel chair with a leg rest filled it even more, and Miss Turnbull, leaning on her crutches, blocked the desk.

"I saw Mr. Lovell," Tippy began—and then she saw that Peter's bag was gone. "Oh, dear," she almost wept, "he's been here."

"What?" Miss Turnbull glanced up, first at Tippy, then at the empty spot her eyes were fastened on. "Oh, I sent it out," she answered. "It's in the girls' locker room. Will you please tell me what you did with all the memoranda I left you?"

"It's—has Peter been here? A tall man who stands very straight and puts his hands on his hips and sort of ducks his head when he looks at you? He has very straight gray eyes and a determined chin."

"My dear child." Miss Turnbull stopped piling up papers into an untidy mass and said irritably, "This is a business office. No young man has been in so will you please find the notations I need?"

"They're here." Tippy skirted the wheel chair and opened a drawer. "Right here," she said, "where we always kept them. And now, if you please, I'd like to go to lunch. The set's all ready from last Friday because they used Studio Two and the auditorium for the talent show. I know it's only eleven o'clock but I have a very important engagement," she finished childishly, losing her fine efficiency and being a worried Tippy again.

"Um."

The answer might have meant permission or it might simply have expressed Miss Turnbull's puzzlement over her own handwriting, but Tippy accepted it as an affirmative, and slipped her purse from the desk.

Her retirement from the business world would have to wait. " 'The show must go on,' " she quoted to herself, traversing the corridor again. "Little people are just little people, after all, and if I were trying to get the hang of things after a vacation, I wouldn't want some sappy little dope bothering me and making it harder."

She combed her curls in the locker room and checked on Peter's bag. It bulged in a corner beside the long mirror, a masculine note that was out of keeping in a place of perfume and lipsticks, of chattering girls who talked of clothes and "fellahs." Tippy lugged it out and set it by a divan in the gray-and-gold reception lobby. Then she seated herself beside it and prepared to wait.

Miriam, the switchboard girl who was partially concealed behind an ornamental counter, sent a wink across the room, and Tippy grinned and sent one back. "Off for the day?" the operator called in her normal voice, before she turned to a woman and said with exaggerated courtesy, "Yes, modom? May I help you?"

"Just for a couple of hours." The woman was on her way to the auditorium and a half hour of quizz entertainment, so Tippy asked, "You haven't seen my young man around, have you? The one who came in last Thursday?"

"Nope. Wait a minute, here's a call for you."

Tippy went across the room and lifted a receiver on the desk. "Tip?" the familiar rumble said. "Something just came up and I'm not leaving till two. Is that all right for you?"

"Of course."

"I know you're busy. See you around one-thirty or so."

She dropped the telephone back into its rest. Miriam's eyes were curious, but she only shrugged as she walked to the elevators and firmly pressed a button. She would go up and pay an unprecedented call on her father.

The radio station of WRIP was as busy as its television neighbor. Tippy found Colonel Parrish in his office, reading news bulletins that had just come in over the teletype, but he looked up from his work and smiled at her.

"Good morning, little stranger," he said, holding out his hand and drawing her to him. "Did you have a good week end?"

"Wonderful, in some ways." She leaned against him and kissed the top of his silvery hair. "How's Mums?" she asked.

"Missing you, as usual, but busy with the rest of our tribe. The MacDonalds and junior Parrishes were over to dinner last night, complete with children. We drove up to see son Robert in the afternoon and took Switzy with us, and Trudy baked one of her famous cakes and sent it up to Bobby. That's all the news I have. Now give me yours."

"Oh, Dad." Tippy pulled up his stenographer's chair and sat down to face him. "I've decided to quit," she said.

"Because of Peter?"

"No." She shook her head and sighed. "Sort of because of him," she amended. "Not that he'd care one way or the other, but because—oh, it's all so mixed up, Dad. I want the kind of life Alcie has—and Carrol, and Penny, when she isn't working. I wasn't *me* all during the week end. I don't

145

belong any more. I was just a—just a younger edition of Miss Turnbull."

"We didn't want you to take this job, Tippy."

"I know you didn't." She got up and walked to the big, plate-glass window with its magnificent view of New York. "It was good for me then," she said, looking down on buildings that would have been gigantically tall in any other city. "I needed something to make me stop thinking and thinking of Ken. This seemed to be the place for me, but perhaps it isn't. I'm still unhappy. I'm still—unsatisfied." She sighed again and turned to face him. "Do you think I've become a problem case?" she asked.

"I think you're about the dearest, sweetest child in the world," he replied. "Come here, a minute."

He beckoned to her, and Tippy went into the protective circle of his arm again, while he said, "Little girl—or 'child,' as Trudy calls you, or even 'childie,' which I heard Peter say when you and he were packing the car—you're very dear to all of us."

"Not to Peter." The words came out and Tippy wished she had them back. "He has his own life, Dad," she said, to make them sound less serious. "Everyone has, but me."

"Because you rush at things too hard. Sometimes," he said fondly, smiling at her, "you make me think of Switzy trying to remember where he's hidden a bone and running about in circles—to the rosebush, back to the hollyhocks, behind the garage. Don't hurry so, Tippy. You're our youngest. Life and love will come to you."

"I don't want love." Tippy pulled away from him and sat

on the edge of his desk. "I just don't want to work for Miss Turnbull any longer. Do I have to?"

"Silly child, of course not. I think you're taking a step in the right direction."

"I wish I knew where it's going to lead me," she groaned. "Just what direction would you say it's going?"

"You'll soon find out." He leaned over and took her hands in both of his. "Good hunting, Tippy," he said with a twinkle. "Now would you mind departing? I'm very busy."

He gave her a little tug and she stood beside him again. "It's funny," she said reflectively, "but you have a nice way of always propping me up. I must be an awfully spineless sort of girl. Everybody's always shaking me into action. Even Peter."

"Especially Peter," he answered, reaching for his reading glasses. "Scoot."

Tippy went back to the elevator and down to the street. She ate an early lunch that she didn't want and hurried back to the studio. The fat canvas bag was still where she had forgotten and left it, and Miriam said, as one conspirator to another, "He hasn't come yet. Turnbull's been having fits because you left, but I stalled her."

"Thanks."

Tippy knew Miriam's eyes would pop if she added, "It's the last fit she'll ever have over my bowed head," but there was time enough for that. She pointed to the bag and was about to ask for its continued protection when Miriam startled her by saying:

"Congratulations."

"What for?"

"I hear you're going to get married. Right away? Don't answer till I plug in a number."

There was no danger of Tippy answering. She was speechless. She watched Miriam push in cords and pull out others in dazed silence. And when all the lines were crisscrossed for communicators to converse with the proper persons, Miriam pushed back her chair and leaned her arms on the counter.

"Well, give," she said. "All the girls are in a twitchet. I said I knew the man."

"Has Miss Turnbull heard?" Tippy held her breath and was afraid to listen for the answer.

"Search me. Maybe. Oh, drat that board." She turned away again, and Tippy took the chance to flee.

The office was empty, the wheel chair was gone. That meant Miss Turnbull was rolling around in Studio One, having "fits" as Miriam said. There was nothing to do but brave her, so she climbed the stairway again.

It didn't occur to her that Matilda Turnbull might be glad to have her leave. Through circumstances, unavoidable but opportune, Tippy had been promoted. And she had done quite well. The technicians said so, the cast all said so, and Mr. Lovell was unsparing with his praise. And she hadn't taken the small part which had offered such a convenient chance for her removal. Miss Turnbull had recommended her for the part. One might say she had presented her to Mr. Lovell as a gift, wrapped in compliments and tied with strings of effusive adjectives. But Tippy had refused the part.

Miss Turnbull, sitting in her wheel chair and eating a solitary lunch, looked upon the entering Tippy with a doleful eye. No news of an impending marriage had reached her. "It's about time you came back," she said. "It's almost one o'clock. Hand me that pickle I dropped, if you please."

"I meant to come back sooner." Tippy bent for the pickle and laid it on a white napkin that covered Miss Turnbull's lap. "Have you heard any—news about me?" she gulped and asked.

"Of course I have. I arranged it."

Miss Turnbull meant the part in *A Lantern of Love*, while Tippy referred to the embarrassing rumor of marriage.

"Well, it isn't true," she gulped.

"I know that, too."

"But I do want to leave. Just as soon as I can."

"Leave?"

"If you can find someone else to take my place. I—I'm not going to be married, but I want to quit."

"Well!" This was pleasant news indeed, and Miss Turnbull took prompt and satisfactory advantage of it. "Mr. Floyd and I have discussed the matter," she said, sounding much more pleasant than she had a moment before, "when I thought you would accept the part. Any girl would be foolish not to," she pointed out. "Though if you're planning to give up a good career for marriage. . . ."

"I'm not."

". . . You would naturally want to leave. So he has offered to lend me a very satisfactory girl from the clerical department. She has done your work while you were away today, so you are free to go at any time."

"*Now*, you mean? Right now?"

"At once, if you like."

"Oh, Miss Turnbull." Tippy's shoulders drooped as she stood looking down at a ham sandwich, a deviled egg, and the pickle she had retrieved. Then she raised her eyes to study the sharp features before her, as she said, "I didn't mean much to you, did I?"

It all came clear. She knew too much. Miss Turnbull didn't want her. "I was really being fired," she went on, "when you tried to give me the other job. That's really the way it is, isn't it?"

"I'm sure I don't understand you, Miss Parrish."

"I think you do. We both understand. That's the way business is, Miss Turnbull," Tippy answered softly. "I guess that's why I don't like it. I wanted to leave, and I planned to, just as soon as you could find someone to replace me, but you wanted me out of here, right now. I'm awfully sorry. Good-by."

She held out her hand, hesitantly and not quite sure it would be taken, not even sure that such a farewell was correct between subordinate and superior, but Miss Turnbull laid down her sandwich and covered it with both of hers.

"You're a nice child, Andrea Parrish," she said. "You don't belong in this cutthroat entertainment world. I envy you, and I wish you every happiness."

"Thank you."

Tippy turned and walked away. She passed the record

room where a strange girl was learning the files and went down the iron stairway for the last time. Girls she had scarcely known looked up from their work to smile at her because they thought she was entering a world they secretly yearned for; and she told herself ruefully, "I didn't make much of a splash when I was just part of the machinery. Now look at me—when they think I'm dripping orange blossoms."

Peter would be coming at any minute. A good-by would have to be said before he reached the talkative, effervescent Miriam, so she hurried across the lobby and tugged the big bag outside to a new resting place on the marble floor before the elevators.

With a whole summer afternoon ahead of her, she could take Peter to his train. Yet here she stood, nervously watching the green lights above her that flicked on and off as cars came up and passed her floor, ready to thrust his luggage at him and hurry him off. Once she would have told him the joke. Once she would have said, "They think I'm going to be married. I said so in order to get out of a job I didn't want, and Miriam thinks you're the groom. Isn't that the most ridiculous thing you ever heard of?" Now she waited and hoped Miriam would have her back turned when one of the elevators opened its doors.

CHAPTER XII

IT was a long week, the one Tippy spent with nothing to do. It was even hard to stay in bed after a quarter-to-seven.

"Seems like you're at kind of loose ends," Trudy remarked one morning, coming down and finding her preparing her father's breakfast. "Why don't you drive in with your papa and buy a new dress? Labor Day week end's coming up and a new fall dress would be mighty nice to have. Move over, child, so I can turn the bacon."

"I don't know what I need a dress for," Tippy grumbled, reluctantly yielding the fork she held. "It's still hotter than the hammers and I doubt if I go anywhere."

"Mr. Peter's comin' back, ain't he?"

"He says so. He's called up every evening—at seven o'clock on the dot, sort of between his engagements and when he thinks I'm home from work—and he says he'll be back. He says he's having a 'very interesting' time. A very interesting time! Well, I'm not. And it's all his fault," Tippy complained glumly. "I was doing fine until he came along."

There was a low chuckle behind her that turned her around to the stove again. "Oh, I know I didn't like my job," she said, glaring. "You aren't being funny. I didn't like it, but I went every day, didn't I?"

"You sure did, child. You done fine."

"And now look at me. I'm browner, when the summer's almost over, and I can whack a mean tennis ball, when I haven't anyone to send it back to but the side of the garage. Oh, I'm leading a lovely life. 'Very interesting', as Peter says."

"You're comin' along pretty good. Run tell your papa to hurry."

Tippy stalked back up the stairs. She could hear her mother's voice behind a closed door, full of laughter and good, morning happiness, and it made her more lonely. "The happy Parrishes," she muttered. "The family everyone says is such a wonderfully happy one. I suppose I'm the exception that proves the rule." And she called aloud, "Breakfast, Dad. You're running late."

"Coming."

She walked on and into her room. At least there was a bed for her to make and some dusting to do. She pulled covers back, then stopped. The two photographs looked back at her from the dressing table, and she walked over to stand before Ken's. "I guess you understood, didn't you?" she said, sitting down before it and crossing her arms. "You knew I couldn't keep on forever, loving you and living on memories. I'm not being disloyal, am I, Ken, because I'm hurt by the way Peter treats me? I'm so confused and unhappy, but I still love you so much." A smiling gaze was her only answer, and she said wistfully, "You told me in your last letter that another love must come to me if you were killed. I think it's come. I don't want it to, but I think it has. I don't seem to care about anything much, right now, but Peter. And he's so changed."

She moved the photograph into a better light, so that it completely hid the one of a boy in a football uniform. "I'll put him out of my mind," she said. "I'll simply forget him. Perhaps I'll go away on a trip and not even be here when he comes back."

A sudden change of mood swept over her. Little sparks of determination glinted like golden flecks in the soft amber of her eyes, as she said, "*That* would serve him right."

But where to go? And would he care? And would she ever see him again? Having admitted that this strange unrest was love, and that all the unpredictable things she had done in these last six days had been done because of it, she was tied as fast and tight to Peter as if he had wound a rope around her. How could she leave?

"I'll go as far as Penny's, anyway," she said in compromise. "If he comes back tomorrow night, at least I won't be sitting at home. I'll go over and ask her to plan a party."

Action was better than the inertia of waiting for a telephone to ring, so she whisked through the housework and asked her mother for the car. For the first time in almost two years Ken's smiling gaze had been unable to help her, but Penny would. Penny would have an answer. She always did.

"Yoo-hoo," Tippy called, stopping her car in a driveway and looking into a side, screened porch that came almost out to meet the gravel. "Pen, are you home?"

Little Parri came around the house, pulling Joshu in an old tin wagon. The children were such perfect duplicates of their mother and father that, except for Parri's hair which was straight brown silk, and Joshu's face, as yet unlined, Tippy had a fleeting impression of Penny and Josh shrunk to miniature. "Hi, darlings," she said, sliding out of the car and hugging them. "Is your mother home?"

"We don't know," Parri answered. And she added in explanation, "We've been on a very long journey."

"All the way to Africa," came from Joshu. "We killed a alligator. He's in here with me. Want to see him?"

Tippy looked down at a dead toad, and said with a mixture of awe and praise, "He's a very fine trophy to bring home. Are you coming in to show him to Mummy or going on another tour?"

"We're traveling some more," Parri answered, "while we wait for Davy to come over. I have to keep Joshu entertained," she said with great importance, "because he ran a tempater last night. He was awfully sick but he's all right now. Good-by."

"Good-by." Tippy watched the explorers start off on another safari and opened the screen door. "Pen?" she called again, peering through a darkened dining room, across a hall and into a bit of living room visible beyond.

"I'll be right down."

Penny's voice came from above, and Tippy could hear her running across the floor and down the stairs. "I was paying bills," she said as she came out, retying the belt of her crisp cotton dress. "I always get so pulled apart when I do it. How are you, pet? That's a cute brown cotton you have on. I like the white collar and cuffs, and the full skirt over a crinoline. It seems to me that you look more rested."

"I feel like Rip Van Winkle after his long sleep," Tippy answered, dropping onto her favorite bamboo *chaise longue*. "I'm not disturbing your work, am I?"

"Mercy, no. It's a pleasure. What's on your mind?"

She had seen Tippy twice since her retirement from business; once at home with the children running about, and once at a family dinner. There had been no opportunity to ask about the dozens of things she wanted to know, so she said before Tippy had a chance to speak, "I've wondered and wondered about you. How are things between you and Peter?"

"Just like they always were, I guess. He's gone to Washington."

"Yes, I know. You told me. When's he coming back?"

"Tomorrow, I suppose. I was thinking you might like to. . . ."

"Have you both to dinner? I'd love it."

Penny had entertained many young men who came out

from town to see Tippy. She had rounded up a few herself and had paraded them for her little sister like a string of fine race horses to choose from. None of them had seemed to suit, so she said hopefully, "I'll have you both over, Tip."

"Just me," Tippy answered in a small voice. "And anyone else you can find. I'd like to have a date tomorrow night and no one's asked me."

"Move your feet." Penny waited until Tippy's white pumps were doubled back, then sat down on the end of the cushion. "All right," she said, "now tell me. What's wrong between you two?"

"Nothing. Just—nothing. That's the trouble. Oh, Pen," Tippy shook a doleful head and sighed, "Peter's so changed. He isn't Peter at all."

"Don't you think that's good?" Penny leaned forward, her brown eyes soft and understanding. "You couldn't see him the way he was, Tip. He didn't interest you at all."

"Yes, he did. I liked him. I enjoyed him," Tippy contended, "and now I don't understand him."

"Listen, cherub." Penny's voice was very slow and patient. "You thought you loved Ken when Peter was being too good and Peterish. Oh, I know you *did* love Ken," she said, as Tippy sat up to protest the first part of her statement. "You loved him truly. But you were just a little girl, darling. It almost amounted to hero worship. Do you think you and Ken could have had a better life together than you and Peter can?"

"I don't know." Tippy laced her fingers together and an-

158

swered, looking down at them, "It almost frightens me *because* I wonder about that. I did love Ken. I do."

"I know it, cherub." Penny drew up her knees and leaned toward Tippy's bent head, saying earnestly, "You have to face things. You'll never know what life with Ken might have been. You'll never have the chance to know. It might have been very beautiful, or you might each have changed and found someone else before it came time to be married. That could have happened, Tip, as it seems to be happening this summer. Suppose Ken were living—and Peter was here just as he is? What then?"

"I...."

"Think about it, Tip, think seriously," she urged. "You are in love with Peter, aren't you?"

"Yes, I suppose I am. If being jealous and frightened over losing him, and not wanting to be with anyone else means I'm in love, I suppose I am."

"Were you ever jealous and frightened over Ken? When he was in Germany and you were here, I mean?"

"Why, no." Tippy looked up and said simply, "I didn't expect him to give up dates and not be with other girls. He was an officer."

"So is Peter," Penny reminded.

"Yes, but it's different." Tippy's head went down again as she said with a sigh, "He always wanted to be with me, before. He never dated other girls. He wouldn't even have looked at Christy once, or gone to Washington, or—or anything. I don't think he—loves me any more."

"Poor lamb, you're in a terrible state." Penny stroked

159

Tippy's curls and said tenderly, "It's awful, the suspense and waiting. Believe me, I know. I thought I'd die if Josh didn't tell me he loved me."

"How did you get him to say it?"

"I popped the question myself, right in front of a store window full of fish and lobsters. He said one little thing that made me know, and I had to."

"I don't think I could." Tippy shook her head and decided soberly, "He might turn me down."

"Just as you've done him dozens of times. Oh, Tip, buck up," she scolded. "If you want Peter, get him. You can't go on being droopy and having him think there'll never be anyone for you but Ken. Look at his side of it. Have you ever encouraged him?"

"Not very much."

"Have you ever made him feel you need him?" Penny persisted. "My goodness, Josh knew I couldn't breathe without him. Why, I'd have begged, 'Don't go to Washington; or, if you have to go, marry me and take me with you.' I couldn't have *let* him go without me."

"Ken's buried in Arlington," Tippy said, her voice low, her head still down. "I haven't been to Washington since you and Dad took me down."

"*Ken.* Darling, stop saying Ken," Penny urged. "Stop letting Peter see you thinking Ken. It hurts him. After all, Tip, I think he's been wonderful to wait as long as he has. I wouldn't blame him if he found someone else."

"I know it, but do you think he has?"

"No, I don't." Now was the time for action. Now was the

time to stick a pin in Tippy and make her jump. Penny believed that the lives of human beings followed much the same pattern as those of the characters in her plays, shaping toward a climax; and since she wanted the third act curtain to come down on a happy ending, she cried, "But I wouldn't take any chances. I'd go after him as hard as I could. I'd put on a campaign that would make the presidential election look like a kindergarten riot."

"You would? What would you do?"

"I'd be at the train to meet him. I'd tell him I gave up my job because I couldn't stand the hours we had to be apart."

"But he wasn't here last week," Tippy pointed out. "The job wouldn't have interfered at all."

"Then I'd say I gave it up because I hoped he'd come back sooner. I'd probably go down to Washington and *drag* him back."

Tippy laughed. It surprised her that she could, but Penny looked so fierce and determined that she felt braver, too. "I can't do that," she said, "because I don't know his address, just his telephone number. But I can buy a new dress and be at the train tomorrow. I can do that."

"Then mount your horse and away! Really," Penny said, jumping up and pulling Tippy out of her cozy sanctuary, where she would have liked to stay and talk some more, "you have a lot to do. Finding just the right dress will take a lot of time, and your hair and nails could stand a beauty shop. Good-by."

"Oh, Pen." Tippy stood in the center of the porch, unsure again as she pleaded, "Do you think it will work? I came over here all set to go about things in a different way, being proud and unavailable, you know, and now you have me grabbing at him. I don't think I can."

"Oh, dear. Sit down again." Penny gave her a backward push that was meant to put them both into battle formation, but Tippy side-stepped.

"I'll try," she said hastily, knowing further argument was useless when Penny planned a course of action. "I'll try everything anyone suggests."

"And my suggestion's sound. Look what it did for me! Look at Carrol and David. Carrol didn't snag our wonderful brother by saying 'go away, I don't want you around!' Your little friend Alcie didn't get her Jonathan by giving him the brush-off and dating Bobby. Look at all of us and remember it takes two to bring about a marriage. We all have husbands, don't we?"

Tippy considered that as she drove slowly along. She felt Penny was right, but she wished she had the opinions of others. Bobby might know how a man would feel about a girl pursuing him, but he was in class. Carrol might have a different approach she could use, not so flagrantly bombastic as Penny's, but this was her day at Red Cross. There was no one else; not even her mother, for a bridge foursome would soon arrive for lunch.

Tippy stopped at the crossroad and sat holding the wheel while other cars skirted her or whizzed along the highway to New York. She felt keyed-up. Like a soldier marking time and afraid he wouldn't start off on the right foot when the command came for the column to march. Right foot, left foot, forward march. "Well, here we go," she said suddenly, and jerked the car onto the highway that led away from home.

Alice didn't live so far away. Peter was her brother. She should know what he thought and how he felt. If he had another girl, Alice would tell her. "Oh, I'm so sorry," she would say, and Tippy would know. And quit hoping. And live forever alone.

With all the cut-offs and the broad new Turnpike, it wouldn't take too long. In a couple of hours the suspense would be over. Tippy pressed hard on the gas pedal and began to plan.

CHAPTER XIII

Tippy felt released as she bowled along toward Alice's brick house in Pennsylvania. And when the speedometer touched sixty, she told the countryside, "Here comes battling Parrish into the ring—Knock-'em-out Tippy, or whatever kind of name prize fighters use. Slugger Jordon, you haven't a chance."

But she slowed at the narrow lane cutting off from the highway and almost crawled the remaining mile. When Alice's property came into view, she began to rehearse her opening speech. "I just dropped by," she said into the wind-

165

shield mirror, and giggled because "dropping by" meant a drive of over a hundred miles. "I gave up my job and was so terribly lonesome," seemed a better approach for a guest who had left just a week ago today, and she decided to use it.

But Alice's house was sound asleep. Blinds were half-drawn like drooping eyelids, and the front door was closed and locked. "Oh, dear," she groaned, seating herself on the front step to wait, and wondering what she should do. Such a long drive back, with nothing accomplished. Alice ought to be at home on a Monday afternoon! This was washday in the country, the day one cleaned and scoured after Sunday. Alice wasn't running true to form—or at least not true to *A Lantern of Love's* schedule. Grandma Bascomb always supervised the work of the younger set on a Monday.

But it was nice in the sunshine. It was three o'clock and the leaves made a pattern on the porch. Late roses smelled delicious, and bees buzzed lazily about, fussing a little because winter was on its way and they weren't quite ready for it.

Like Christmas, Tippy thought, with lazily drifting thoughts. No one is ever ready for Christmas, not even on the eve before. Or for love, or—or anything.

She closed her eyes in the quiet solitude, peaceful, her hands hanging limply between her brown, full-skirted knees, and she had forgotten even Peter and all her problems when she heard the honk of a horn.

"That's Alcie," she said to a butterfly on the trellis beside her, sitting up and looking. "She honks at everything, even at shadows. She drives by sound."

A car turned in and she prepared to rise and begin her speech. "I gave up my job," was as far as it went, for she saw two heads in the car. One was Alice's, beyond a doubt. The other. . . . She froze on the step. The other was Peter's.

There was no chance to run, for her own car blocked the driveway better than a bulldozer. It sat up there like the Statue of Liberty, its New York license plates proudly proclaiming its out-of-state status, and it brought another surprised squawk from Alice's horn and a spurt of gravel from her sliding tires.

Both heads looked through the windshield, then turned to each other. Tippy could see them. She could even see the look of surprise on two faces; and in her misery, she thought they registered annoyance. Then Alice's door flew open and she sprang out.

"Why, Tippy," she called. "How long have you been here?"

Now was the time for her speech. "I just dropped by," she shouted, and discovered she had started the wrong one. It didn't even answer Alice. "I mean," she corrected, "I've been here about half-an-hour."

She wished she could sink out of sight. Just vanish. Here came Peter, looking astounded, and there stood Alice, with her feet apart and her eyes staring at a ghost on her sacred premises. "It was such a nice day, that I—that I took a drive," she stammered.

Peter had almost reached her, and sudden anger struck her a mighty blow in the chest. What right had he to be here? "Well!" she said, and jerked her shoulders back. "If it isn't our Washington friend! How are all the little men in the Pentagon carrying on without you?"

Peter stopped at the step and looked up at her. "Golly," he said, "I never dreamed of seeing *you*. You *are* real, aren't you?"

"Touch me and see," she retorted, vowing she would slap him if he did. "I'm very real. And I'm just starting home. It was nice to have seen you--in such an unexpected place."

"Tip." He moved just enough so she couldn't push past him as he said, "Alcie met me at the station and was going to put me on a later train, but can I ride up with you?"

"You most certainly may not. We have a date for tomorrow."

"Couldn't we make it tonight?"

"I'm busy tonight. I'm busy *every* night!" she blazed. "Will you kindly *move* yourself?"

Penny's council that had sounded so sensible flew out of her head. Who was she to collapse on a man who was somewhere where he had no business to be? Here he was with his *sister!* That meant he had come to see his sister's *sister-in-law*, of course, and it was no wonder he was stunned to have his plans go wrong. Christy might be coming, any minute.

"Just move," she stormed," and let me down from here. How can I get past you when you stand there like a block of wood?"

"Do you really want to go by? I can leave if you want to stay."

He stood looking up, his gray eyes puzzled and two little creases between his brows, like someone happily come to a

168

party and met with a rebuff at the door. He looked so wistful, so honestly surprised, so hurt, that Tippy stared over his head. Where, oh, where was Alcie?

Gone. Faithless Alice. The lawn was empty. "I—I . . . oh, I think you're horrid!" Tippy wailed. "You're deceitful and horrid—and—and deceitful!" And with that she collapsed on the step, her face buried in her lap.

Let him see her cry, it didn't matter. If he could make out the words that came through her hands so much the better. "I'm tired of being nice to you," she sobbed, "whenever you don't want to be with other girls and p-people. I wish I had my job back. I wish I'd taken the p-part in the darned old p-play. I will, if Penny asks me again. Maybe I'll be famous someday, and you'll be s-sorry you treated me any old way."

"Tippy. Oh, childie," Peter said softly, sitting down on the step and putting his arms around her, "I don't want to hurt you, not in any way. I didn't mean to come back again and hurt you. Don't you know that, Tippy, darling? I've never wanted to make you unhappy."

"But—you do. You keep coming back and going off—and coming back again—*all at the wrong times!*"

"Which do you want me to do? Stay away?"

"I don't care. Oh, de-ear."

She gave a strangled sob that made him draw her closer. It was hard to hold her, knowing he was going to lose her. He was sure now that she still clung to the memory of Ken, in spite of all he had tried to do, and he said with a sigh, "I'll go away, darling. I want you happy."

"I'm—miserable."

"I know you are. I've stirred up sad memories and inter-rupted your life, but I had to. I couldn't make a life for myself until I came back, Tippy. I had to find out what chance I had."

"You have—lots of chances. There's FECOM and EUCOM, and you can go in any direction you want to."

"Yes, I guess I can." He looked out at the lacy shadows, wondering why go anywhere, if he had to go alone. "Alcie thought you had begun to love me," he said with a sigh.

"I do," she wept, "but she didn't need to tell you. It wasn't fair. Not when you came to see Christy."

"Christy?" He pressed his cheek against her hair and asked, "who's Christy? What's she got to do with it?"

"She. . . ." There was something in his voice, an inquiring wonder, that made her risk lifting her head and letting him see her tear-stained cheeks. "Oh, Peter," she asked desper-ately, "*are* you in love with someone else?"

"Not to my knowledge. How could I be when you're the only one I've ever loved? You're my darling, my childie, my one and only girl."

"Oh. Then wait a minute." A beautiful white light burst over Tippy like a rocket shower of stars. Peter still loved her! "Wait just a minute," she gulped, and bent over to wipe her eyes and cheeks and even her wet trembling lips on the hem of her cotton skirt. "I look so awful," she wept again, coming up. "But I—I love you so much. Oh, Peter, will you marry me?"

Her arms were around his neck and he could hear her sobs that wouldn't stop. It was a strange way to accept a proposal of marriage, but he had to calm her. "Childie, childie," he said as soothingly as he could, above the pounding joy he felt. "Stop *crying*, Tippy! I'd be very happy to marry you."

"I thought I'd lost you."

"Well, you didn't." Another sob burst near his collarbone, and he pleaded, "Stop crying, darling, and let's enjoy this love scene. I never thought it would happen, so *please*, let's enjoy it."

"I am." Tippy clung closer and wailed, "I just can't let you see my face, that's all. It looks so awful."

"It looks like an angel's to me." He managed to pull her chin up and kiss away the tears on her lashes. "You're beautiful, even when you cry," he said with wonder. "You're so lovely I'm afraid you'll vanish."

"I won't. I'll always stay as close to you as this," she sighed, moving nearer. "Oh, Peter, why has it taken me so long to know?"

"Because. . . ." he shook his head. "It has," he said simply. "Kiss me, Tippy."

Her lips came up to meet his in the first real kiss she had ever given him. It was a kiss of love—tender, passionate, and clinging; and it made him know, even more than her words had done, that her heart belonged to him now, completely and without reserve.

"God, make me worthy of her," he prayed as he held her. And it seemed right that he should say a silent, "Thank you, Ken;" for she was Ken's gift, given in death, to be loved and treasured.

He wondered if Tippy could be thinking that, but when

he looked into her eyes they were happy and serene. "I love you, I love you, I love you," she said. "I love you so much I had to ask you to marry me. Now you ask me."

"Darling," he said, still a little serious in his joy, but hoping he sounded humorous, "will you do me the honor to become my wife?"

"Oh, yes." She sighed and leaned back against him. "Penny said for me to pretend I need you terribly," she told him happily, "but I forgot about it. I was so mad and jealous I forgot. But it doesn't matter, I do. I'll tell you now. I do."

"Wha-hoo!" He let go of her so suddenly she almost toppled over. "Wha-hoo!" he shouted again, springing to his feet and raising his arms to the sky. "She *loves* me!"

He went leaping off the step, tore around in a small circle and back again, as if he had started a race and won it, while Tippy laughed and watched him. "You idiot," she said. "If you're so excited about a little thing like marrying me, why didn't you ask me before you went off and wasted a week in Washington?"

"I couldn't. It had to come from you."

"But why?"

Her upturned face was honestly asking; and he put his foot on a step and leaned toward her, his arm across his knee. "Suppose I'd kept on plaguing you, Tip," he said, "and one day, just from boredom or because your job had gone sour or something, you'd said yes. How would I ever have known you loved me? How could I have been sure?"

"I suppose you couldn't have been," she said thoughtfully, thinking back on those terrible months after Ken's death, when she had poured out her grief to him. "Are you now?"

"Yes." There was just a flicker in his gaze before it met hers steadily, and he smiled. "I'm very sure, but I'm not taking any chances. I'm going to tell Alcie and have a witness. I'm going to yell it all the way from here to your house. Hear ye, hear ye," he cupped his mouth and shouted. "Four o'clock and all's well. Andrea Parrish and Peter Jordon have plighted their troth. Come one, come all."

Alice bounded out to the porch, showing she had been hovering near, and Tippy cried, "Why, you snooper. Aren't you ashamed!"

"I didn't look and I didn't listen," she protested, hugging Tippy as she scrambled up and flinging herself on Peter. "I just stood in the back hall and prayed. And I even stopped that long enough to take my only steak out of the freezer. We'll have the engagement party tonight."

"Hm-hm, we can't." Tippy pushed her away, saying, "Unhand him. He belongs to me now." She looked up at Peter from inside the circle of his arm to ask, "Would you mind very much if we go off by ourselves? I'd like to ride along and plan, and I want to tell Mums and Dad and the family, and I want to make up for the silly time we've lost."

"Good-by, Alcie."

Peter would have started off but Alice caught his arm. "We didn't decide about the children," she said, laughing. "I inherit Susan tomorrow and have to outfit them all for school. You're supposed to make the rounds and talk with their teachers."

"Can't possibly do it. I'm too busy with my own delayed affairs." He pulled Tippy in front of him, his arms around her waist, his chin resting on the top of her hair, and requested, "You do it, Alcie. Get Christy to take 'em shopping with you. She's a good scout."

Tippy tipped back her head and looked up at him. "She's a vampire," she said.

"And man's best friend." Peter kissed the tip of her upturned nose. "As soon as I get to New York, I'm going to send her a present."

"Why?"

"Because she aroused your jealous instincts. Did you know," he asked, grinning down at her, "that Chris took time out to give me a rush? Alcie told me she'd asked her to."

"I think that's awful! Alice Drayton, I'm ashamed of you," Tippy scolded, leaning out of her cage. "I owe her an apology. I was terrible to her. Every time she came near me I wanted to hit her." She pulled Peter's locked hands apart and marched up the steps, as he called:

"Where do you think you're going?"

"To call up Christy," she answered, her dimples working. "To tell her I've got you and—well, sort of thank her." Then she whirled around and ran back down again. "No, I won't," she decided. "I'll call her tomorrow. I'm too busy today. I'm too happy. I couldn't talk straight. Let's go."

Alice walked across the grass with them and opened the door of her car so Peter could take out his bag and transfer it to Tippy's sedan.

"There's that thing again," Tippy laughed, as the mound

of bulging canvas plopped out at her feet. "When I was dragging it all over the studio, I never thought I'd be so glad to see it again. Nice old fellow," she said, leaning down to give it a pat.

Peter stood regarding it, too. He rumpled up his short yellow hair while he made a momentous decision, then squatted down and began unbuckling its straps. "Alcie," he invited while he tugged, "go get Tippy a coat. No, never mind," he called as she started off. "I've a trench coat she can use if it turns cool. Just fade away."

"And please telephone Mums and tell her where I am," Tippy called, as Alice started obediently off without a backward glance. "Put it in collect."

White shirts, khaki shirts, ties, and shoes tumbled out on the grass before he found a brown leather shaving kit. "Kind of a funny place to keep my valuables," he said, unzipping it. "Well, what do you know!"

Tippy knelt down beside him to see what he had found. A small box fell open and dress studs and army insignia spilled out, but he pushed them aside. "This little baby," he said, snapping open another lid, "is what I'm looking for. Isn't it lucky that I'd just happened to have it along with me?"

Tippy looked down on a miniature West Point ring. It matched the one on Peter's hand, in a daintier, smaller way, and it had the same engraving around a deep blue sapphire that was the stone his class had chosen. "It looks—as if it might belong on a girl," she said in a very small, awed voice. "Oh, my goodness, I do wish it would fit me."

"Care to try it on for size?" he asked, taking it out of its white satin bed.

"If it fits, may I keep it?" she held out her finger and watched the ring slide on. "Oh, may I, Peter?" she breathed. And they sat down on the lawn, amid the welter of his clothing.

CHAPTER XIV

"WE forgot to tell Alice good-by," Tippy said, when they were driving along the cross-country highway.

Her head rested on the back of the seat and she made high, ostentatious gestures so that her new ring flashed in the sunset.

"Alcie won't mind." he answered, "and don't distract the driver."

"Do I?" She moved a little closer and asked, "Shouldn't we start planning now? We've been engaged for almost half an hour. We can't just go on and on with no plans, because I don't believe in long engagements."

"What have you to suggest?"

"That we get married. Right away. That I go back to Texas with you."

"Woops, wait a minute." Peter slowed the car and looked at her bright face turned to his. "Fresh lipstick and dimples become you," he said, wishing he could kiss her again. "What about your job?"

"That?" Tippy snapped her fingers. "I gave it up the day you left for Washington. I'm free as air," she said. "What about yours?"

"That's one of the things we'll have to talk about. I suppose our whole life will have to hinge on my job. On ours," he corrected, "since an army career and an army family are one and the same."

"We'll be a family." Tippy turned her head again and studied him. "That seems funny, doesn't it?" she said. "It always seems natural for Mums and Dad to be a family, they've been one ever since I've known them, and had to move around in the army, but it seems queer to think of us having responsibilities."

For a second something skipped a beat in her heart and her eyes went shut. She saw, clearly and fleetingly, dinner for two in a Washington hotel. Ken smiled across the table while she pretended she had cooked the food they ate. Then she laid her hand on the rough tweed of Peter's sleeve and asked, "Where will we start being one? In Texas?"

"I don't think so. I'll have my orders soon—and, Tip, I've decided to go to EUCOM."

"Oh, golly, I'm glad. I can go to Turkey with you, can't I?"

"When I go, you can, but not right yet." He fished a package of cigarettes from his pocket, shook it and pulled one out with his lips, while she pushed in the dashboard lighter. "I took advice from everyone I could," he said. "And the army seems to be going in strong for career planning. I have to have troop duty, so I'm going. . . ." He leaned to the glowing coils she held, said, "Thanks," and went on, "I'm going to Germany, Tip, for a year or so."

"Oh." She knew what he wanted to ask but was afraid to say, so she had to say it for him. "You think I wouldn't want to go back to Germany, Peter, don't you? Well, I would. I didn't like it when I was there with Mums and Dad, I hated it, really. Except for the times when Ken came down to Garmisch, it was awful. But you see," she said quickly, as much for herself as for him, "I won't be lonely this time. I'll have you. When do you have to go?"

"In about a month. How would you like," he asked, "to be married just before I'm due to leave, and fly to Europe on your honeymoon?"

"And not marry you right away and go to Texas? Oh, Peter."

She sounded so disappointed, so like a little girl who had been promised she could stay up late and then was sent off to bed, that he grinned and explained, "I was a very smart fellow when I only took fourteen days of a thirty-day leave. I saved out some in case I could come back and get me a bride."

"But I don't want a big wedding," she pouted childishly. "I want to go to Texas with you and then come back to New York with you, and go to Europe. I want it all."

"Tippy." They were almost at the toll gate that blocked their way to the Turnpike, and he pulled to the side of the road and stopped. "You aren't afraid, are you? Afraid you'll regret your promise? You aren't trying to do this quickly, so there'll be no turning back?"

"I'm afraid I'll lose you," she protested. "I'm scared stiff of every girl in Texas. Anybody who could flirt with Christy the way you did, would be a snap for some scheming girl. I'm afraid to let you out of my sight."

"Then if that's all it is, you can relax."

This time he did kiss her. He let other cars speed past to pick up mileage on the nonstop run to New York while he did it; and when he had put the car in motion again, he dropped the piece of cardboard a uniformed guard passed out from his window.

"A little nervous there, mister," the guard said, picking it up and pushing it in to Tippy who reached across for it. "Just married?"

"In a few days." She nodded and smiled at him. "We just got engaged today," she confided. And she leaned around Peter to ask, "Are you married?"

"Six kids."

"How nice." The car gave a lurch and she banged the back of the seat. "Good-by," she called, and borrowed one of Peter's hands from the wheel. "That man in there doesn't remember me," she said, "but I turned in my ticket and paid my money to him coming down, and I thought he was sort of glum. It shows that it was all in the way I felt, doesn't it? Now let's plan some more. When we get out to Texas, where will we live?"

The drive was a long, happy argument that ended only when the car turned into the Parrishes' driveway and Switzy came tearing out like a black cannon ball shot into the night.

"Oh, you cute, loyal lamb," Tippy cried, stooping over and letting him lick her face. "You're going back to Germany and have a daddy." She looked up to ask anxiously, "You wouldn't mind his going with us, would you, Peter? Even if Ken gave him to me?"

"Of course not, childie. Switzy belongs with you. Here, boy."

Switzy wiggled away to leap up on him, and Tippy watched Peter caress the little dog. "I suppose you know you're very wonderful," she said, linking their arms together. "We will now enter the house and announce our honorable intentions. Switzy, lead the way."

Colonel and Mrs. Parrish were playing double solitaire at a bridge table set up near the open door to the terrace, and they looked up with surprise. "We thought it was Josh and Penny," Mrs. Parrish cried, jumping up and sending cards in all directions as she flew across the room. "Oh, Tippy, darling, Alcie told us, and we're so happy for you."

She gathered Tippy into her arms while Colonel Parrish's hand shot out to Peter. "Good for you, son," he said. "I had a feeling, from the way this girl's been acting lately, that you were on the right track. I might say we expected the news."

"Thank you, sir." Peter gripped the offered hand and answered with a shy grin, "I wouldn't have taken any bets on it, myself." He bent his head for Mrs. Parrish's kiss and laughed when Tippy stuck out her lower lip and complained:

"I think you're a terrible bunch of people—conniving

behind my back. And Alcie should have let me tell my own parents. By the way," she asked, trying to sound stern as she frowned at Peter, "Why did you stop off at Alcie's and waste more valuable time?"

"Because I couldn't stay in Washington any longer. I thought Alcie might buck me up," he said easily; and he teased, "You didn't give her a chance."

"I won't give anyone a chance after this." Tippy pulled a little away from the group and stood with her feet apart, her hands clasped behind her back, as she announced valiantly, "I intend to marry you in three days. Just as soon as we can get our license and take blood tests." And she turned to her mother, admitting, "We've argued and argued, all the way home, but I'm going to."

"No, Tippy, don't," Mrs. Parrish begged with frightened emotion. "Be sensible, darling. Don't rush us into losing you. Be married as Penny and David were, with something lovely for us to remember—unless, of course, Peter can't come back again."

"Oh, he can. The very provident lieutenant," Tippy retorted indignantly, "saved out fourteen days."

"Then let's have a wedding. Please, Tippy. Just a simple one in the Governors Island chapel, where Penny was married and all the children have been christened."

But Tippy shook her head. It was useless to tell them she had lost one love, that she couldn't risk losing another. She could only say, "He might be killed on a plane going to Texas or coming back here. I want to be with him." And all through the evening, not even the combined arguments of

Penny and Josh, or the quiet pleading of Carrol could sway her.

"Listen, you little dope," Penny fumed, when she had distributed hugs and the news of a rushed marriage had been broken to her. "Your wedding day only comes once, so you might as well have something to look back on. It's fun. It's wonderful. It's ten times more exciting than just walking into some justice of the peace's office." And she knelt down before Tippy to say, "It's beautiful. It's so solemn that you know you're married for keeps and forever. Carrol, come here and talk to her."

Tippy was stubborn. She looked up at her beautiful sister-in-law, seeing her serene, calm loveliness, and went right on with her plans. "I'll admit you were the prettiest bride I ever saw," she finally said. "I was just a little thing, but I hoped I could wear a veil someday and look exactly like you. I used to dress up in an old lace bedspread of Mum's, and practice. But now," she hunched up her shoulders and declared, "I'd rather look like me. I'm not the bride type."

"Then do it for Mums and Dad, kid," David answered her, coming over to scowl down and order, much as he would have done his two young sons. "Give them a break. If they want to spend the money, the least you can do is let them."

"I'll save them money." Tippy laughed up into his blond good looks. "They can take a trip on it; they can come visit me in Germany. Now isn't that better than blowing it on a wedding? Really," she said, looking around the room, "you're the silliest bunch of people I ever met—and that

183

includes you, too, Peter. Anybody might get the impression you don't want to marry me."

"After five years of waiting?" he inquired. "From the time you were a sophomore in high school? I want you."

"There, you see? It's settled. Peter has spoken." Tippy tried to push out of her chair past Penny. "I do cause more discussions in this family," she sighed. "You're always having to gather together and do something about me. I thought this was supposed to be a party. People always laugh and act frolicsome at an engagement party."

"Then go out and bring in the cake Trudy baked in a hurry," her father said, stubbing out his cigarette and pulling his face into a happy mask before he turned around. "There's ice cream, too, I believe."

"For that I'm thankful!" Tippy cried, patting her chest, then moving her hand down to a proper location on her stomach. "We ate like fury in a restaurant on the Turnpike because we were in such a hurry, and I'm starved. Fiancé, come help me."

She managed to squeezed past the glum Penny who squatted like a statue of The Thinker, her flowing skirt spread out on the floor; but in the darkened dining room she stopped and put her arms around Peter's neck. "Do you mind very much being married as soon as we can?" she asked, standing on her toes.

"Oh, childie, childie," was all he said. And he buried his face in her curls.

Trudy was sliding the cake onto a silver tray when they pushed open the door, so she set it down on the table and held out her hands. "It's a happy day for all of us," she said. "I've been hearin' the ruckus goin' on in yonder, an' if my littlest one don't act just right, Mr. Peter, you'll have to forgive her. She's the onlies' one we have much trouble with."

"I'm the onlies' one who knows what I want." Tippy laughed and handed Peter a silver bowl filled with ice cream. "You can set that on a table," she ordered. "then come back for a stack of plates, and spoons and forks." And she said to Trudy as the door closed again behind him, "I sounded just like Alcie. Isn't it fun?"

"It could be, if you takes it right."

Trudy went back to arranging her cake and Tippy laid down the napkins she had picked up. "Now what do you mean by that remark?" she asked. "It was something important, because it always is."

"I was just thinkin' of Mr. Peter," Trudy answered, removing a piece of icing that fell on the tray. "It's kind of too bad for him."

"What is?"

"Marryin' him so quick."

"But why?" Tippy stared. "He wants me to marry him this way. He said so."

"Somehow, child, I don't quite think he does."

Trudy's eyes were soft and tender; and Tippy stared into them, her face suddenly pale and her lips trembling as she remembered Peter's words when she had first suggested this quick marriage.

"Maybe he's thinkin' the same as I is," Trudy said. "Maybe he'd rather wait and have you know your mind."

185

Tippy stood in silence. She rubbed both hands down along her cheeks and held them there. Peter had said, "You aren't afraid you'll regret your promise, are you?" And in the dining room, he had only answered "Childie, childie." It had sounded like a groan.

"Oh, Trudy," she wailed, "what have I done?" and turned and flung herself at the swinging door.

"You win," she called from the hall, plunging on. "We're going to have a wedding. It's what I want so don't start asking questions. I simply changed my mind, that's all." And she rushed straight at Peter, smiling up at the glad relief on his face.

CHAPTER XV

LIGHTS were out downstairs and the house was quiet. Tippy stopped in the door to her room and leaned against the frame. Switzy was sound asleep in his basket, and the glow from a lamp on the table cast loving shadows over the familiar furnishings. She had something to do.

Very softly she closed the door and sat down before her dressing table. The two photographs were where she had left them that morning. Ken still hid Peter; and she said to him, "Darling, it's all come true. I'm happy, Ken. It's Peter. Someway, I have to make *him* know I'm happy. Even if I have to put you out of my life, and my sight. Oh, Ken."

She took the photograph up and laid it against her heart. For a long moment it rested there, then she held it away and looked into the face she knew so well. "Forgive me, darling," she said, and walked across the room to a low bookcase along the wall. Pictures of her family were grouped along its top: her mother and father, delicately tinted; Bobby in disreputable tennis clothes; her nieces and nephews on their tricycles and a pony; Penny, in her latest play; Carol; David; Josh; and Trudy, snapped on her way to church. She set Ken's photograph in the midst of them so it held a valued place and wouldn't be lonely. Then she left it quickly to open her door and go back along the hall.

"Peter?" She called softly, tapping at the little sitting room where he was to sleep. "Have you gone to bed?"

"Not yet." He opened the door and came outside, without his coat and tie. "I just started undressing," he said "Something you want?"

"You, for a minute."

She led him down the hall and stopped where she had stood, looking into her room. His eyes rested on the dressing table, on the one lone photograph. From many previous visits, he knew that Ken's picture was gone. "What is it, Tippy?" he asked "What are you trying to tell me?"

"That I love you. That there's no one else in my life," she answered. "I want you to believe me, Peter, because it's true."

"I believe you, darling."

"Sometimes," she said slowly, "and I'll have to tell you this, because it will happen—a familiar song, a flower grow-

188

ing on a mountaintop, the way someone uses his hands, will bring back memories. But they'll only be fleeting, Peter, and tender, and not touching us. They'll be just—tender."

"I know that, childie. I wouldn't want you to forget Ken," he said. "It's right to keep everything that's good in our lives. We have to have our memories."

"So I put his picture over here, with all the other ones I love," she pointed. "He lives with them now. You and I . . ." she leaned against him and smiled at their reflected faces in the mirror ". . . are going to be a family, just like Mums and Dad."

"Is this why you changed your mind about the wedding?"

"I didn't want you to have any doubts. Oh, Peter, you mustn't, ever."

"I never will again."

"Because I truly wanted to go with you." Here was someone she could bare her heart to. Here was someone to whom, for all the rest of her life, she could bring her troubles and griefs as well as her joys; and she said, "I'm so afraid to have you away. Not like this afternoon when I was afraid some other girl would snatch you, but because so much can happen to a person when he's away. You see, it happened to Ken. And I'm afraid, Peter. I'm terribly afraid."

"You needn't be. My arms will always be around you. Why, I'll take a slow freight back if it will make you any happier. Or better yet, suppose we change our plans again and you go with me?"

But she said in a resigned voice, "No. Mums and Dad are so happy, this way. And I have to learn to be trusting. I can manage for a couple of weeks," she told him, looking up, "if you'll be very, very careful."

"I'll step around my own shadow."

"And after we're married I can watch over you." She pulled his face around to kiss him, then stood up straight and laughed. "Right in plain view of that couple in the mirror," she said, clicking her tongue against her teeth. "Dear, dear."

"They were kissing, too. I saw them."

"I wonder if that girl's as happy and hungry as I am," she laughed. "Getting engaged is so exhausting that I haven't eaten very much today."

"I could do with a snack. I could do with anything that would keep us down in the kitchen for an hour or two."

He swung her around and they went along the hall, their arms around each other. Switzy, contented in his basket, opened a sleepy eye and saw them go. His beloved was leaving him. In the middle of the night. Just when they always settled down. Duty called, so he opened his mouth in a wide, pink yawn, then padded faithfully along behind.